Shaking Hands
with a Tarantula

Alan Addison

D1428561

Shaking Hands with a Tarantula

ISBN:
ISBN-9781983375187

DEDICATION

This book is dedicated to my brother William Addison for always being there for me and without whom nothing would have been the same.

Shaking Hands with a Tarantula

CONTENTS

Glossary
Scots language is used by a few characters in the book. If
this language is not one of yours, there is a Scots-English
glossary at the end of the book. You can also find Scots
language dictionaries on the world wide web.

Shaking Hands with a Tarantula

ACKNOWLEDGMENTS

Some say that elders can learn from the young and I agree wholeheartedly. Consequently, I wish to thank my grandchildren for their ideas about the title and cover design.

Shaking Hands with a Tarantula

CHAPTER ONE

Tuesday 4th November 2014

The invitation to the Literature Salon Event had come at Tod like a bolt out of the blue. He'd neither seen, nor heard from Mhairi, the ex-colleague who'd invited him, since his days as an adult literacy tutor. That felt like a long time ago, even though it had only been a year since he'd been forced into early retirement on the grounds that he'd been caught receiving class-A drugs. Tod had never taken drugs in his life, but that was another story.

Tod and Mhairi had been on the same post-graduate course at Moray House and had got on quite well, when he did the listening. Still, he thought, while giving his brown brogues a polish for the first time in months, the free wine and nibbles must be worth it, if nothing else.

He'd hardly been over his own doorstep since the Fort Case had hit the headlines back in September. All hell had let loose then, though JP Associates had so far remained out of the picture. Bob James, Tod's partner in the investigation agency, was keeping an even lower profile and Tod wondered if this might be to do with Bob's girlfriend and JPs funder, Rebecca Stark. Rebecca would be struggling to cope with her beloved Uncle Peter's name being splashed across every tabloid, and the few remaining spread sheet newspapers in Britain. He wondered if she, like most, suspected that it had been Bob who'd got that ball rolling.

Although Edinburgh was in the grip of another cold spell, the Bar Austen was awash with literati, and others, commonly termed in Leith "the hangers-on", the minnows happily swimming atop the big fish inhabiting the murky waters of publishing success. When he entered the bar, Tod recognised a few of the faces, but no-one seemed to recognise him as he made his way towards the free wine. No sign of the nibbles, though many there looked satisfied enough. He did spot Mhairi and was pleased to see she was engrossed in conversation with someone he took to be a like-minded lover of books, most likely for babies. She was too engrossed in her subject to notice him.

After his first sip of the wine, he began wondering why he'd bothered to make the journey up from Leith and made an instant decision, threw back the warm wine and took hurried steps towards the exit, just as a familiar face appeared from the opposite direction.

'Well if it isn't Mr Peterson!' exclaimed the Reverend.

'What brings you to this neck of the woods?'

'Reverend Mackie,' said Tod, shaking his hand. 'I didn't take you for a writer.' The Reverend Callum Mackie, recently retired minister of Tod's parish and Leith Parish Church, was now serving as pastor to the seamen who had the good fortune, or misfortune, depending which way one looked at it, to find their ships moored in Leith Docks.

'It's a mysterious world, this world of ours, Mr Peterson. I am, contrary to your opinion, penning a wee story about the exploits of the seafarers who have graced our shores over the last century, or three. I was told this was the place to be if one wanted to meet the right people, and here I am meeting you. Are you in the writing game by any chance?'

'It's Tod by the way. Can I get you a glass of wine Rev...?'

'Wine? Me? No!'

'Sorry, I forgot,' said Tod eying the dog-collar.

'I'll hae a wee dram though. I wouldn't touch the grape with a bargepole. Isn't Tod the old name for the devil?' The Reverend smiled and shook Tod's hand again. 'Callum will do nicely.'

The Reverend had never seen Tod in his church but had met him a time or two in his capacity of Community

Education Worker and had heard about JP Associates and their last investigation into the Fort case. It had been the minister's friend, William Norman, who had witnessed the young student take an object from the body that had been discovered on the Fort archaeological dig.

'I see your agency managed to get its name in that foreign newssheet,' said Callum.

'Pardon?' asked Tod.

'The Glasgow Herald: something about an on-going investigation into political espionage related to the body they found during the Fort dig.'

'I can't say anymore on that subject, Reverend, or I'd have to kill you.'

'Just remember I'm well protected lad,' said Callum, looking up at the ceiling.

'What, you've got a minder in the attic?'

'Something like that,' laughed the Minister. 'Am I getting that dram? I'll have a Singleton if they have it.'

'It won't be free,' said Tod, not sure how much a good malt would cost him. 'It's only wine that's on offer.'

'It will be free for me,' laughed Callum again.

Tod was getting the drinks in, for the third time, just as Detective Sergeant John Mackay was tearing his small, black, unmarked police car around another bend in Edinburgh's New Town. His passenger, retired Detective Inspector Bob James, sat next to him.

'For Christ's sake John, slow down, my arse is beginning to feel as if I'm on a bucking- bronco.

'Sorry Sir! It's the cobbles, they play havoc on the suspension too,' replied John, as the car rocked and screeched loudly into Great Kings Street.

'Where in heaven's name did you learn to drive like that Son? It wasn't from Police Scotland's finest, that's for sure,' complained Bob, trying to hold onto the dashboard.

'Sorry Sir, I thought you knew; I drive rally-cars at weekends; it's my hobby.' John suddenly slammed on the brakes. 'He's dumped the bike and gone down that lane.' The young officer was pointing down St. Stephens Street Lane.

Having agreed earlier in the year to act as consultant to Police Scotland's Cold-Case Squad, Bob didn't think for one minute he'd find himself giving live chase to a suspected scooter thief. He'd imagined that most suspects, and perpetrators, would be gone to pastures new. 'John, I think it would be better if you lightened up with the "Sir". You know what our leader thinks about that, now I'm retired. We wouldn't want to upset

Detective Inspector Sandra Laing now, would we?'

Most of the budding writers, agents and literati had disappeared from the pub just about the same time as the free wine had dried up. Tod and Callum were leaning on the empty bar staring at the gantry. Callum still hadn't put his hand in his pocket. 'I've a wee liking for the Glenkinchie too,' he said.

'I'm a McCallans man, myself,' said Tod, hoping to inspire his new friend into putting his hand in his pocket.

'So, are you fancying another wee drink?'

Tod thought his luck was in. 'Is the Pop...,' he stopped before finishing his reply.

Callum smiled. 'It's just some of my transient parishioners are having a wee party down on their ship in Leith Docks. It's the Captain's birthday and I'm invited. I was wondering if you'd care to join me.'

'Is it one of those oil-rig supply ships? That's all that seems to come in to the docks now, though the Royal Yacht came in, but it never got out again.' Tod's father had been a merchant seaman and had sailed out of Leith during the war years. It still bit Tod's craw that the docks had been taken over by the oil industry and tourism.

'It does involve the black stuff, but not oil. Believe it or not Tod, some cargo still finds its way to Leith. It's a merchantman carrying coal.'

On their way through Edinburgh by taxi the two men were in full-flow about the happenings and changes that had taken place in the city.

'Have you ever seen so many cafes in your life?' asked the Minister. 'The leisure and pleasure gods are most certainly amongst us.'

'We get more and more European by the day,' replied Tod. 'Café culture, I believe they call it.'

'Aye, and the patrons all singing the devil's mantra, "A cannae be bothered".'

'What's your point,' asked Tod, looking out on the busy scene.

'The world of work, the one you and I belonged too, is God's creation. Have you read Augustine on the subject?' Callum didn't wait for a reply. 'Leisure, and all it entails belongs to Beelzebub. Sloth, nothing more than Sloth. It was Sloth that led to the fall of Rome and Sloth which has become our God again. In his adopted name, leisure, people have stopped cooking for their bairns; they've stopped helping their neighbours, but they'll find time to go to their leisure-centre or gym and walk on the treadmill, going nowhere.' He pointed out of the cab window. 'Look, there they sit in those cafes, with their wine or cappuccino, as if the world belongs to them. It may look social, but people are no longer living communally, and it is the worship of leisure and all it entails which is swallowing them up. Most of them are on anti-depressants. No Tod, the word leisure belongs to Sloth and you see his work all around you.' Callum swept his arm across the scene.

Tod was beginning to wonder if he'd maybe got himself involved with Rasputin and if he'd been wise in agreeing to come to the party. Either that or what Callum believed was exactly what was happening to people. Tod had seen it in his work in North Telford: many parents had stopped cooking for their bairns and any sense of communal living had long disappeared as far as he could tell. Friends lived on social media now. He doubted though whether he could have put all that down to leisure being the work of the devil. More likely a system keeping people in their place, the old status quo raising its ugly head again.

As their taxi passed through the dock gates the first thing Tod noticed was the all-night casino. He wondered what the Reverend would have to say on that matter. He didn't have long to wait to find out.

'There's another example of our leisured society Tod, only that one has dreams attached, dreams of even more leisure, if one could but win enough. Aye, he's all around us now my boy,' Callum sat back against his seat 'and no more so than here in Leith.'

'I hope you don't mind me saying Callum, but don't you think it a bit far-fetched to think the devil responsible for all the failings of post-modernity? Don't you think that capital and commerce is as at the root of it all? Give folk more time to themselves and they've more time to spend on goods and on social media, where they'll see yet more ads for more goods.'

'You've a point there. I've often thought that given a life of leisure, one has nothing to talk about, unless of course one can develop an alter ego that speaks of and for you. Social media is the tool that takes care of that. Not to change the subject, and talking about spending one's time, the men you are about to meet spend most of their time in some of the worst weather the Almighty can throw at them. They are braving the wild oceans for a pittance of a wage and yet most of the money they earn goes home to the Philippines. Not one penny finds its way to the leisure palaces we've just passed on our way here.'

'You said earlier their ship carries coal. Is that for our power stations?'

'Aye, it is that. Longannet is still burning away over the Forth there in Fife, though Cockenzie coal-fired Power Station in East Lothian has been decommissioned and that's where their coal used to go.'

'Is it Colombian?'

'What?' asked Callum.

'The coal. Because if it is Colombian then the chances are it is from the Cerrejon open-cast mine that is creating so much mayhem with the local population: farms shut down, people put off their lands. Some call it dirty coal.'

'No, it's not from Colombia. I do know quite a bit though about South America and its recent economic relationship with Scotland. Did you know we play our part in Petrobras, the Brazilian oil giant that's knee deep in controversy? What a silly question, of course you do. In answer to your original question though, these lads have been delivering coal from North Russia. It might be just as dirty as any other fossil fuel but the crew that brings it here, these Pacific Islanders are facing the wild seas of the Arctic to bring it here to heat your house and they're sending all their hard-earned pay back home to their families. You wouldn't get many Scotch laddies doing that now, would you Tod?'

'Scots,' said Tod, 'I think you'll find the word is Scots.'

'I thought you were a literature man? You haven't read much on Albert Mackie then my boy, have you? Oh aye of course, you studied at one of yon English Universities, Cambridge was it not? You wouldn't have learned much Scotch writing down there. "Speak Scotch, or Whistle", that was Bert Mackie's mantra.'

Before Tod could ask more about Bert Mackie and his use of Scotch, the taxi drew up on the dockside adjacent to an old cargo ship, which did not look as seaworthy as Tod expected. The thought immediately struck him that being on such a small vessel in the rough seas of the Arctic would not be the easiest of professions. Once more he thought of his own father on the Arctic Convoys.

The two men walked down the sloping gangway onto the ship and were welcomed by a very merry crewman, who, it appeared, had already had a few. Hugs and hand-shakes over, Callum introduced his new companion. Tod was given the same welcome. Once inside the ship it could not escape Tod's notice that some of the crew were dressed as women.

'Don't worry,' whispered the Minister, 'It's just to liven things up a bit.'

'Liven things up a bit?' asked Tod.

The two men remained on board the vessel until the early hours of the morning and may have stayed longer, had the crew not had to prepare for sea later that day.

CHAPTER TWO

Wednesday 5th November

When he woke later in the day, Tod did not have much memory of the Captain's party, having been subjected to what he could only describe later to his friend and business partner Bob James, as some of the best hospitality he'd ever come across. He didn't mention the women's dresses that half the crew had worn to liven the night up.

One thing he did remember from the night was that he had been escorted from the party rather the worse for wear, by the First Mate. He'd left the ship's company as Callum was saying his fond farewells to them. It was obvious from the handshakes and hugs that their pastor had built a great rapport with his seagoing parishioners and that they in their turn trusted the Minister explicitly.

Escorted by the First Mate, Bayani, the first thing that threw Tod the landlubber off kilter was that he was looking down at the dockside from whence he'd come a few hours earlier. Bayani spotted his confusion. 'The tide is in and we are now above the dock.'

The two men had leaned on the guardrail of the ship and stared out across the docks. Tod remembered Bayani speaking about his life at sea and his family back home in the Philippines, before suddenly changing the subject. 'There are many opportunities that exist for illegal trading at sea but not for us, the coal ships coming into Grangemouth and Hunterston.' As he spoke he focussed hard on the large oil-rig supply ships that filled the docks. 'It's a different matter with those monsters of the deep.'

As far as Tod was concerned those ships were home-grown and only involved in the North Sea oil industry, 'But those ships just ply their trade between here and the oil-rigs in the North Sea, don't they?'

'Those monsters are not merely supply ships. Their cargo may look like supplies for your oil-rigs but there is something buried deep in their holds, something that no-one sees and no-one talks about, but it is there, and it is coming into your country from lands far from here.'

Tod had been about to question Bayani further when Callum came on deck.

'Well my lad, it's about time we were heading off. These men have an early start tomorrow.'

'Right.' Tod shook Bayani's hand. 'Got to go, and thanks for the party, and the shipping lesson.' He was about to walk onto the gangplank when he remembered he was now ten feet up from the dock. Moving slowly, he'd followed Callum down the narrow gangplank, hanging on to the chain-link grab rail for dear life, when the minister stopped in his tracks and turned to enquire about Tod's parting words to Bayani.

'Oh that,' Tod had answered, 'it was nothing really.'

'Nothing? Nothing comes of nothing my boy.'

'He was just telling me about the oil-rig supply ships.'

'Oh!' Callum had answered. 'So, you'll be going off in search of one grand, white, hooded phantom then Ishmael.'

'You know your literature Reverend, if you don't mind me saying?

'As you know your devils, Mr Peterson.'

CHAPTER THREE

Thursday 6th November

Big Jake was sitting on his bench at the end of the Kirkgate when Tod arrived, even though November had brought with it weather to put off even the hardiest of Leithers.

'I see the morning frost hasn't deterred you from your reveries Jake,' he said as he sat down on the bench beside him.

'A'm taking every opportunity A can; the council are planning another revamp at the bottom of Leith Walk, and A suspect ma bench might be in line for the chop. So, what's up?'

'Nothing's up. I just thought I'd pop along and see how you are. Would you like a coffee?'

'No thanks. Young Mark has just been over with one.'

Tod knew that Mark le Mot, PhD Psychology student and JP Associates' part-time researcher always brought Jake a coffee when he was on shift as a waiter nearby. He also knew from Jake's somewhat frosty welcome that the big man was still smarting from what he, and the other affiliated members of the team saw as a rebuff during the last case. 'How is Mark?' he asked, 'I haven't seen him since our last case.'

'Your last case?' commented Jake.

'Do you not think it's time you got over that Jake?'

'Over what?'

'That last meeting we had in the office. I apologised to you all then, didn't I.'

'Aye, so you did Tod, so you did.'

'And I meant it.' Tod looked directly at Jake.

'How is ex DI Bob James getting on?' asked Jake. 'Is he still pining after his posh tottie?'

'I think we all know Rebecca well enough to be able to stop calling her his "posh tottie", don't you?' Tod had always defended his life-long friend, now business partner Bob, but surprised himself by defending Rebecca.

'Now don't get all defensive on your friend's behalf Tod. How's Tracey? Is she still managing to hold down her job, working for you intrepid sleuths?'

Tracey had been secretary to Tod and Bob almost from the moment they'd set up JP Associates Investigation Agency in Great Junction Street, a one-minute walk from where Tod and Jake now sat.

'It's nearly a year already. She seems to be holding her own, though she says she is missing you and to pass on her regards.'

'It beats me how the lassie puts up wie the two of you. Is she still making the tea and going the messages?'

'Right Jake, how many times do you want me to apologise for not being a team player? I think "control freak" was how it was put at the meeting. That last case was just too complicated and too dangerous to have you, and the others, any more involved than you were. It was for your own good, all of you!'

'I didn't know you cared, or if you'd noticed we've all grown up. Well, all except Harry that is, and maybe we can decide when we wish to be involved and when we want out.'

Tod sighed loudly. 'Okay I accept that and have apologised! Now, can we move on, please?'

At that moment, a passing drunk tried to join them on their bench. Jake put out his left crutch to bar his way.

'Awright big man, nae need tae be like that. A only wanted tae take a weight off,' slurred the stranger.

'Well take it off somewhere else!' answered Jake. 'Ma friend and I are just about tae discuss some business.' He turned to Tod. 'Isn't that right, Mr Peterson.'

Tod smiled, knowing from Jake's reaction that he was forgiven. He was glad of that because Jake, alias the

Oracle, knew more about the goings on in Leith than any other. Tod waited until the drunkard had gone his reluctant way before continuing. 'I wanted to ask you something Jake.'

Jake smiled. 'Surprise, surprise.'

'What do you know about Leith Docks, and its links to the oil industry?'

'Well the recent news is that they've found a body down there, by Victoria Quay,' answered Jake.

Jake's reference to JP Associates last case, and the discovery of a body that turned out to be that of an MI5 agent, threw Tod off guard.

'That's now in the hands of the press. We've no idea how our Glasgow cousins got wind of the story, but they did, and you know what they're like; the proverbial dog with a bone.

'A think A might have a wee inclination whae spilled those beans, but we'll say nae mair about that. What dae A ken about the oil game and Leith Docks; where dae ye want me tae start?'

'The beginning would do,' said Tod.

Jake explained that he'd a cousin who'd skippered a tug-boat, prior to his retirement the previous year, and who'd worked in the docks all his life. Leith Ports Authority, the owner of the docks, had made a euphoric rise to fame when it bought docks in London and now owned most of the ports in Scotland. Rumour had it that Leith Ports was a mere trading name for a multinational fund manager. As far as Jake's cousin was concerned though, Leith Ports had been a good employer and he'd left with a good pension.

'So why do you want to know about the docks?' Jake asked.

'No wonder they call you the "Oracle",' said Tod. 'Someone I met the other night implied that the oil vessels docked there may be hiding a dark secret, though I suspect it is more likely just another sailor's tale of the deep. Do you think it possible?'

'A cannae imagine how sailing between Leith and the North Sea oil platforms can raise much hope of buried treasure, can you? Unless of course you're talking about the scrap metal that comes off the rigs. That's worth an absolute fortune tae those in the know. But then you're the conspiracy theorist Tod, A'm sure you could come up wie something.'

'The chap was from the Philippines; maybe they are prone to hyperbole,' answered Tod.

'What's that, some kind of sea monster?' asked Jake,

'Never mind,' replied Tod, 'never mind.'

CHAPTER FOUR

Friday 7th November

'I don't care how short-staffed we are, when I agreed to join your Cauld Case Squad as consultant I didn't expect to find myself being driven by Stirling Moss in a car-chase around the streets of Edinburgh.' Bob pointed over at DS John Mackay. 'I've only just managed to get my spine back into shape.'

'Oh, poor Bobby, are you not up to the chase anymore?' answered Bob's boss, Detective Inspector Sandra Laing,

Bob was still smarting from having been ordered to escort John to apprehend a known thief and to being subjected to John's rally driving techniques.

'It wouldn't be so bad, but we didn't even catch the bugger!'

Sandra Laing left her desk and walked over to Bob's. 'What's wrong? You can tell Auntie Sandra. Is it Beccy again, has she not been in touch? How awful.'

'This has nothing to do with Rebecca and I wish you'd stop referring to her as "Beccy", if you wouldn't mind,' said Bob, who was still in the throes of trying to forget all about Beccy. But it wasn't working, and Sandra knew that.

'Something is sticking in your craw Bob, and if it's not

Beccy, what is it? And don't give me the stuff about the car-chase.'

'You were in the drugs squad before you took over here Sandra, weren't you?'

Sandra couldn't know what was coming, but she already had that sick feeling she got every time Bob James introduced a new subject. She didn't even want to ask, but she did.

'Why do you want to know?'

'Were you ever involved in any drug related incidents regarding illegal imports when you headed up the drug's squad?'

'Oh God, give me strength!' She lifted both hands to the ceiling. 'Don't tell me, your resident conspiracy theorist has been at it again, put two and two together and come up with three hundred. Remember we agreed that your involvement with JP Associates creates a conflict of interest, and that is not on the cards.

'Would you listen to yourself Sandra, this has nothing to do with Tod. I was only asking, and conflict of interest or not, it appears that JP Associates has been aiding and abetting your rise to fame recently, what with the Jane Keen case and the Fort case.'

'I don't remember any satisfactory conclusion with the Fort case. Do you know something I don't Bob

James?'

Bob realised he'd said too much. 'Can we leave that aside for the moment. I only wanted to know the recent history of drug imports and you were the leading light back then. That's all.'

'You'll be telling me next you weren't out for a wee dram or two with that pal of yours last night and the subject didn't come up. No don't even bother to answer that, I surrender! For your information, I have been involved in import related drug offences recently, the biggest of which was the confiscation of Cocaine worth £30m seized in the River Clyde ship raid. More than 100kg of cocaine was found on that ship. That was back in May. We swooped as the ship waited to dock at Hunterston after arriving from Colombia. It is not the first bulk carrier to arrive in Hunterston with more cargo than its crew expected. Three years ago, the then UK Borders Agency found 10kg of cocaine in the hold of MV Bulk Australia as it delivered another load of Colombian coal in the Ayrshire port.'

'I had heard something about that but didn't know you were directly involved.'

'Aye, they wanted an expert to join with agencies from England and the Netherlands, so they came to me. Anyway, does that answer your question about drugs and imports?'

'Near enough.'

'Okay spit it out. What else do you want to know?'

'Anything untoward ever occurred related to the oil game?'

'Right Bob James, enough is enough. What is this really about?'

'Well not much really. You were right, it was Tod who brought up the subject. He'd been at a party on a ship in Leith Docks and one of the seamen mumbled something about things being hidden in the holds of the ocean-going oil-rig supply ships. He couldn't have told his tale to a more receptive audience. Tod told me about it last night and I said I'd run it past you, as you are our resident expert on illegal imports.'

'Aye right,' replied Sandra. 'Well you can tell your pal Tod that apart from very small stash finds on oil-rig workers during the occasional strip-search by HM Revenue and Customs, there's nothing else to report. I'm afraid your Joseph Conrad will have to find his heart of darkness elsewhere. I hope he is not too upset by your findings and please pass on my regards.'

'Now you don't have to be like that Sandra. I was only asking. And by the way, I didn't know you were into literature.'

'I'm not, but Margaret is. She's studying with the Open University for an Arts degree. And for the record, the last time you asked me one of your innocent questions, I ended up in front of the Chief, trying to explain why I'd interfered in a case that we'd been told was off-limits, remember!'

'Aye, sorry about that Boss. Imagine your Margaret studying the arts. She could ask Tod to give her some hints and tips, he's an Arts man.' Bob turned his attention to his computer.

'Never mind the "your Margaret" Mr James. I don't want to hear any more about this nonsense. Now, get me those statistics on the Stewart case. I asked you for them over two days ago.'

'I'm all yours,' said Bob, switching on his computer.

That was the morning of Friday 7th November. By late afternoon that day Bob was back with his friend and business partner Tod leaning on the bar at the Starbank Inn.

'So as far as Sandra is concerned your seaman's tale is a work of fiction. In other words, you're up a gumtree.'

'What I find strange though is that the Reverend Mackie implied, after Bayani's revelation, that I'd go searching for a grand phantom.'

'He maybe knows you better than you think, said Bob, 'We all know that you are partial to a grand, hooded phantom or two.'

Tod took out his mobile phone and began texting.

'Don't tell me, you've a direct line to phantom world?'

'The next best thing. Callum and I exchanged mobile numbers and he likes a wee dram, or five, so I thought I'd see if he could join us and you can get it straight from the minister's mouth. I hope you've got a full wallet with you because when Callum starts talking it's difficult to shut him up and he talks for Scotland.

'Oh no, not a Minister, not on a Friday night. Folk don't like them boarding their ships, apart from Filipinos it seems, and some folk don't like them in pubs either, including me.'

'The text bounced back almost immediately. **Aye, see you shortly.**

When Callum arrived, he was dressed in old, tattered track-suit bottoms and a baggy, worn, country-style checked shirt.

'You didn't need to bother getting dressed for the occasion Reverend,' said Tod, as Callum approached.

'You caught me in the conservatory, right in the middle of dead-heading my pelargoniums, giving them their prep for winter.'

Bob's face lit up. 'You grow pelargoniums?'

'I do that,' answered Callum. 'You must be the infamous Detective Inspector Bob James I've heard so much about.' The Minister put out his hand.

'Just plain old Bob James, since last December,' replied Bob, shaking the minister's hand.

'I'm very pleased to meet you Mr James.' He turned to Tod. 'So why the invitation? I can't quite remember the last time someone invited me to join them in the pub; the dog-collar normally puts them off.'

'You could give Monty Don a run for his money with the garb you're wearing tonight though Minister,' said Bob.

'When my parishioners call, I'm happy to down tools, no matter what I'm up to, especially when a wee dram might be in the offing. And forget Minister; like you, I'm retired so it's just plain old Callum.'

'What type of pelargoniums do you grow?'

'I nurture the Arctic Star mostly. Coincidentally, it shares the name of the medal given to the merchant seamen who braved the North Sea on the Arctic Convoys during the war. I've some African Violets too, a hint of the exotic. Are you interested in plants Bob?'

'Aye, I've a collection of pelargonium myself. I go for the reds and have quite a collection.'

Tod couldn't believe his ears. His own father had been on the Arctic Convoys but hadn't received any medal, though he'd lost many friends. Even more shocking than that, he knew nothing about Bob's interest in growing flowers.

'I've gleaned most of my learning from Gardeners' World and Beechgrove Garden and I keep my pelargoniums in the courtyard at the back of my flat. It's touch and go whether they survive the winters,' said Bob, obviously warming to the Callum's company. 'I'd die for a conservatory but don't have the space.'

'You'll just have to keep them covered up in winter; you can buy special sheeting to cover them,' said Callum.

'Excuse me for interrupting gents but what should all good gardeners be doing on a night like this?'

'Oh aye,' answered Callum, 'I'll have a Macallan and a half-pint of Landlord.'

'I'll have the same,' said Bob, smiling from ear to ear.

Once Tod had got the drinks in and had handed them round, he walked away from the two men, glad to leave them to their in-depth discussion on the mesmerising qualities of the pelargonium. He found a window seat and sat with his back to the view across the Firth of Forth. He still found it hard at times, watching this dark river which had played such a terrifying role in his

29

nightmares. Even the mention of the word "red" by Bob when describing his pelargoniums took him back to the murder of Brian Hopper and the bloodied knife he'd left protruding from the boy's side.

He looked at the two men leaning on the bar and couldn't remember the last time he'd seen his lifelong friend Bob so engrossed in conversation. Both men were using their hands to mimic what Tod took to be secateurs, cutting imaginary flower stems in the air.

It had been at least two years since Tod had been in his friend's flat in Portobello. At that time there was no sight of flowers, nor any other sign of nature in the flat or garden. The only things of note in the place were the case charts and photographs lining the walls: murder case notes and macabre photographs. The courtyard of the Georgian flat was merely a haven for insects and birds, long grass and weeds growing through the cracks in the broken paving. Bill Oddie would have liked Bob's nod to conservation, Tod had thought at the time. Which was why Bob's conversion to gardener was a complete surprise to Tod. Now he realised they were both capable of keeping secrets from each other. The only difference was Tod couldn't discuss his with anyone and nor could he produce, imaginary or otherwise, the tools of his recent hobby.

Eventually the men decided to join Tod and looked around to find him.

'Callum was just giving me the nitty-gritty on taking cuttings and dead-heading,' said Bob as they placed their drinks on the table and sat down.

'This is a new one on me Mr James,' said Tod. 'You certainly kept that quiet.'

Callum saw Bob's face changing colour to a light pink and intervened. 'Everybody needs a wee hobby Tod, you of all people should know that, and there is nothing more fulfilling than helping make God's creation become even more beautiful. But I digress, that is not why you contacted me, is it?'

'No, it's not. I was discussing with Percy Thrower here,' he pointed at Bob, 'the revelation of the first-mate on that ship – remember the story involving the grand, hooded phantom, as you so succinctly put it. I thought you might be able to shed some more light on the subject for Bob's sake.

'It's nothing,' replied Callum. 'I don't know what else I can add to Bayani's story, except to say you've got to take those tales of sea monsters and the like with more than a pinch of sea salt. I've heard the same sort of stuff myself in relation to those oil ships or "monsters of the sea" as they are known by many a merchant seaman. Personally, I think it's probably more to do with the fact that the oil industry has all but taken over the docks and the money involved makes that industry very lucrative indeed, whilst traditional seafaring has all but run aground.'

'Are you saying these rumours are fabricated by merchant seamen and are based on nothing more than envy?' asked Tod.

'Not exactly, but what I am saying is that you must tread carefully before you go charging into another conspiracy theory with all guns blazing,' replied Callum.

'What do you mean another conspiracy theory?' asked Tod.

'Did I say that?'

'You did.'

'Did you ever discover whose body it was found in the Fort, and why it was buried there?'

Callum's change of subject threw both investigators slightly.

'I'll get them in,' said Bob, standing up.

The last thing either he, or Tod for that matter, wanted was to discuss the Fort case. That was one experience they were definitely trying to put behind them.

'I don't know,' said Tod, once Bob had left the table, 'I just got the feeling that what Bayani was referring too was very real. I began to wonder if it might be drugs or some such. In fact, I think I gave Bob that impression when we met up the following night and he was going to run it past his superiors.'

Before Tod could explain further Bob returned with the whiskies and three bags of crisps, which he scattered across the table. 'Take your pick. I thought they might help soak up the alcohol and keep us going till we can get a fish supper.'

'Did you know,' said Callum 'that Edinburgh used to be the centre of the European opium trade in the nineteenth century? Talk about addiction, people couldn't get enough of the stuff back then. Remember Conan Doyle and his Sherlock Holmes, poor Sherlock was addicted to opium, but then Tod you of all people would know that.'

'What do you mean, "me of all people"? I'm no expert on the drugs scene, past or present.' Tod began wondering if the Reverend knew about his previous dealings with the drug pushers who'd stolen Brian Hopper's record book.

'I meant you being a literature man.'

'Oh that, of course,' Tod replied, though still unsure of Callum's motive.

'It strikes me,' intervened Bob, 'if you don't mind me being involved in your wee conspiracy, that what we need is to ascertain whether or not those oil-supply ships could, in any way, be involved in drug trafficking, or any other trafficking for that matter.'

Callum changed the subject. 'Did you know that Scotland's oil and gas supply chain is being urged to take advantage of investment in Brazil's energy projects? Scotland, because of its knowledge of deep sea exploration, is at the forefront of expansion into Brazil's energy markets. Brazilian oil is very lucrative and Scottish Development International, Scottish Enterprise, and Subsea UK, the owners of those "monsters of the deep" are heavily involved.

'And?' asked Bob.

'Brazil presents an excellent opportunity for Scottish business. Scotland has an incredible wealth of energy resources from a range of generating technologies, capable of involvement in exporting those resources elsewhere. As well as the natural resources, we have a pool of skills. It's clear there are great opportunities for Scottish companies in Brazil, and that the skills and expertise built up over the past decades in the North Sea will be of great use to companies seeking to invest.'

'I still don't get it,' said Bob. 'Should we be worried about that?'

'Antonio Claudio Correa from Brazil's national energy company Petrobras has been over having discussions with our industry leaders. There are significant market opportunities for Scottish companies, particularly in the subsea sector. In fact, Scottish Development International have set up an office in Rio de Janeiro to ensure that companies have the support they need to tap into these potential opportunities.'

Bob interrupted. 'This is all very impressive Callum and your knowledge of Scottish industry obviously holds no bounds, but I still don't see what this has got to do with criminal activities, imagined or otherwise.'

'I do,' said Tod. 'Petrobras is involved in scandals and accusations. There is even talk of those accusations, if they are proved to be true, eventually bringing down the Brazilian Government.'

'Aye and with global subsea growth predicted to double from £20 billion to £40 billion by 2017, the international market offers a plethora of opportunities for the scrupulous and the unscrupulous,' added Callum.'

'And I thought Mr Peterson here was a conspiracy theorist. It would seem they are breeding!' commented Bob.

'There are two very serious issues with Petrobras,' continued Callum, ignoring Bob. 'The Brazilian authorities are calling their investigation into the company "Operation Car Wash," and that investigation has reached the highest levels in the Brazilian government. President Rousseff's regime is accused of shaving 3% off the company's contracts in kickbacks to finance her election campaign. There have been reports that she admitted there was a "deviation of public money," though she later denied making those comments. In March a Petrobras former refining head was arrested for taking $400 million from the company. That's a lot of money, in anyone's book. There's also an investigation into Petrobras' $1.25 billion purchase of an oil refinery in Texas in 2006. Authorities in Brazil, the Netherlands, and the US are also looking into $100 million in alleged kickbacks Petrobras gave to SBM Offshore NV, a Dutch company that makes supply ships for the oil industry. Now where do you think these ships may have ended up? Then of course there are the most recent arrests and warrants issued. Many are for high-level executives of construction companies that allegedly gave or took bribes from corrupt Petrobras officials and that's a way of business that Scottish companies may not what to learn from.'

'How did you learn so much about all this?' asked Bob.

'Your friend Tod here knows.' Callum touched Tod's shoulder. 'I'm writing a book about the history of seafaring in Leith and of course, the oil industry must come into that, playing the important role it does now. The company which runs those monsters, for example,' he pointed out the pub window towards the docks, 'has just signed a $1.6 billion-dollar deal with Petrobras for the construction of three pipe-laying vessels. Aye Mr James, legal or illegal, there's big money in the oil game.'

'I think you're reading far too much into this Callum. According to my sources there has been little illegality regarding oil-rigs or ships,' replied Bob. 'But then as you say yourself, there doesn't have to be; they make enough, and that's without the risk.'

Once again Callum ignored Bob's intervention. 'Then of course you've got the coal, most of which comes from Cerrejón in Columbia. Some say it is dirty coal, stained by the blood and sweat of the people of La Guajira. In Europe, people enjoy light at the suffering of these communities. It's said that children have died because of contaminated rivers, and that the mine uses huge amounts of water leaving people dying of thirst. Coal mining in Colombia has led to the destruction of the social fabric and the destruction and disappearance of sacred sites, according to reports. This has not stopped us importing it though and according to British government figures, nearly four million tonnes of Colombian coal was imported to Hunterston in north Ayrshire in 2013. A substantial portion was burned in Scotland's biggest power station at Longannet in Fife.' He turned to Bob. 'You'll have heard about the massive haul of cocaine worth thirty million discovered on a ship moored off the Scottish coast?'

'Aye,' said Bob, 'I was discussing that very recently in fact.'

'Police found 348lbs of the class-A drug in the rudder area of the Cape Marcos, which had sailed from Colombia. It was anchored just three miles from Hunterston, Ayrshire. They also seized diving equipment, a rigid inflatable boat and an underwater "scooter". The ship had set sail from Puerto Nuevo in Colombia loaded with a cargo of coal. As you know, Colombia is widely regarded as one of the biggest suppliers of cocaine throughout the world. The £30m haul of the drug would have generated tens of millions of pounds on the streets after being cut down into smaller-sized deals. Think of the suffering that would have caused.'

'We see that every day here in Leith,' added Tod. 'It also makes you wonder why we ever stopped mining our own coal.'

'Good point,' said Callum, before continuing. 'Then there was a Colombian drugs baron who was considered to be behind 80 per cent of the global cocaine market. He was linked to Scotland's biggest drugs haul, worth £100m.' Callum turned on both men. 'Is that home-grown devil enough for you boys?' He sat back in his chair.

The rest of the evening passed without incident, with neither man saying much more about the comings and goings of seafarers in Scotland. But as they were saying their farewells outside the pub, Bob reminded Tod of the importance of keeping the team on board with his thoughts about Bayani and the sea-monsters. Callum had already wandered away from the two men and was half way up the steep hill that sided Starbank Park.

'Keep the team on board about sea-monsters? You really are a dark horse Bob James. First, it's pelargoniums, then conspiracy theories, and now you're a team player.' Tod looked up the hill. 'He's some character our Callum Mackie, is he not?'

'A bit intense perhaps, but I couldn't help like him. He certainly knows his stuff about economics, the sea and drugs.'

'Yes, and devils too, if you listen to him long enough.'

'Aye, and I think he really has seen his devils,' said Bob, looking up the street.

'What do you mean?'

'Did you check out the old tracksuit he's wearing?'

'No.'

'You didn't notice the badge on the trousers? You're losing your touch. There was a time when you needed to know the meaning of everything.'

'Oh, the badge,' replied Tod, defensively. 'I thought it was the tracksuit designer's logo.'

'Tell me,' said Bob, as Callum disappeared over the rise of the hill, 'does he strike you as a man who would wear a designer tracksuit? No Tod, that logo doesn't belong to any designer; it looks like our Callum may have been a member of the Special Boat Service.'

'Special Boat Service, what's that when it's at home?' asked Tod.

'You've obviously heard of the SAS. Well the SBS is similar, but also deals in amphibious action. And I've heard it said that the SBS is twice as tough.'

'Mm,' mused Tod, still looking up the hill.

CHAPTER FIVE

Monday 10th November

The team meeting which Tod had promised was arranged for lunch-time. Bob thought it best to avoid it because of his involvement with the Cold Case Squad and possible conflicts of interest. His recent rift with Rebecca was another reason, but Tod argued that it was prudent to include her, as she was JP Associates fund manager.

No one had seen her since the break-up with Bob back in September, though Bob claimed it wasn't so much a break up, as more a parting of the ways. It was true, he had abandoned Rebecca during their first weekend away together and had taken the first plane home from London, but that had been very necessary, and Rebecca should have understood that, according to Bob. Tod still felt responsible for the break-up as it was his plea that had brought Bob scurrying home after only two days. If his need had not been so desperate, the couple would still be together.

Rebecca was first to arrive at JP Associates for the meeting. Every other member of the team had answered the call in the positive, which was no surprise after the ribbing they'd all given him about him not being a team player and how they felt excluded from the investigations. They couldn't very well step back now, thought Tod, smiling to himself as he met her at the door.

Harry, ex-burglar turned amateur forensic specialist and computer whizz kid would be there. He would have no choice in the matter anyway as his wife, Tracey, was secretary to JP Associates and she called the shots, well most of them.

Young Mark le Mot, PhD psychology student and waiter in a restaurant at the foot of Leith Walk would be there too, complaining as ever that he'd had to find cover for his shift.

After Rebecca, Jake was next to arrive and looked as if he was happy to be there. He'd been retired from the post-office a while and now spent most of his days sitting on the bench at the end of the Kirkgate. Locals called him the Oracle as he seemed to know more than most about life, past and present, in Leith. Leith Police had other names for him relating to his time as a fence, or middle-man for stolen goods. Jake himself said he merely knew the rhythm of the place.

When the office door opened for the final time and they were all seated around the coffee table, everyone thought it was Tracey back with the sausage rolls and acted accordingly. Mark jumped up to put the kettle on while the other cleared the magazines from the table top. Then suddenly everyone stopped in their tracks and stared. Standing in the doorway of JP Associates was a church minister, dog-collar and all. 'For those of you who don't know me, I'm the Reverend Callum Mackie, retired. I thought you wouldn't mind if I joined you.'

Before Tod could explain their meeting was confidential, Callum cut in. 'You'll be waiting a while for your lunch; I saw Tracey standing in a queue that stretched halfway down Great Junction Street.'

'You know Tracey?' asked Tod.

'Oh aye, he knows our Tracey all right, eh Callum,' said Harry.

'Would someone care to enlighten me further?' queried Tod.

'The Reverend Mackie is on pastoral duty at the jail and guess who one of his clients is? Tracey met the minister there when she was helping Jimmy McGuire wie his English,' replied Harry.

Before Tod could muster an answer, the office door opened again and Tracey walked in with two carrier-bags of hot, savoury pastries. When she saw the Reverend Mackie, she did a double take. 'For a minute there, A thought A was back in Saughton,' she blurted.

No matter how much time had passed since Saughton Prison changed its name to Edinburgh Prison, most people in Edinburgh still referred to the jail as Saughton.

'There's enough hooks, crooks and comic singers here tae fill the jail and you might find yourself back in the clink Tracey, if you dinnae get those goodies on the table,' called Jake.

'That was merely some light relief; I thought you were all going to pass-out seeing a Minister enter your not so hallowed ground. Well, here I am regardless and somewhat peckish myself,' said Callum.

'A didnae get you anything,' said Tracey.

'He can have mine,' said Rebecca, 'I'm not very hungry.'

'Is health food more your cup of tea Hen?' asked Jake.

'No, I'm just not very hungry.'

'Isn't Bob joining us?' asked Callum, looking around the room.

They all kept their head down and no-one answered. Eventually Rebecca lifted her handbag and began rummaging in its depths.

Callum, guessing something was afoot, changed the subject. 'I tried to get Bayani to join us, but they are somewhere in the Arctic as we speak.'

'Whae's Bayani when he's at hame?' asked Harry. 'It sounds like a hot curry.'

'He's a Filipino sailor, and I can assure you, he's not very hot at the moment,' chastised Callum. 'In fact, he and the rest of his friends will be surrounded by ice and freezing fog as we sit here tucking into Tracey's feast.'

'A didnae get you anything,' repeated Tracey.

'Bayani is the reason we're here,' said Tod, attempting to shift the focus from sausage rolls.

After Tod explained the reason for the meeting, Callum went on to describe Bayani's life and how he sends his pay back to his family in the Philippines. Then he talked in detail about Bayani's revelations to Tod on the night of the Captain's birthday party. He completed his long soliloquy with the updates on recent crime in Scotland that could be linked in any way to Leith and the sea.

By the time he'd finished and sat back in his chair, obviously satisfied, he'd covered the main points. His audience, on the other hand, was stunned into silence and thought the best course of action was to offer him some of their food.

After some minutes Tracey broke the reverie by getting up to make a fresh brew.

'So, in a nut shell,' said Tod, 'that's what we've got, a throwaway comment by Bayani about sea-monsters and hidden crimes. Now that may not sound much to go on, but Callum and I believe it might be worth looking into, something worth investigating.'

Harry was the first in with a suggestion. 'A could visit the dock authority's offices.' He thought he'd said this quietly enough for Tracey not to hear.

'Oh no you cannae!' Came her reply from the kitchen. But then Tracey knew her husband well enough to know he'd meant an evening visit, when the offices were closed.

Rebecca was next to try. 'My late Uncle Benjamin's estate left me as shareholder in a great many companies involved in imports. He was a diamond merchant and had a wide range of contacts.'

'A finger in a great many pies Hen,' said Jake, lifting a pie from the greasy bag.

'Those pies, as you call them, are what are feeding you, don't forget that. And please stop calling me "Hen"!' Rebecca stared straight at Jake, knowing it was now or never if she were to be taken seriously by the other members.

'Excuse me Hen, but A'm no relying on yours, or JP Associates pies tae feed me.'

'So, what you are saying is you are no longer involved in our investigations,' said Rebecca, getting everyone's attention as she did so.

Jake was only a hairsbreadth from walking out. 'A'm

starting tae feel like A'm on Dragon's Den!'

Mark, who'd grown close to Jake over the last year intervened. 'Talking about pies, are there any left?' He pointed to the greasy bag.

'As I was saying, before I was so rudely interrupted, I'm happy to make enquiries and happy to continue fund this enterprise, if you so wish?' Rebecca looked to Tod for support.

Tod knew that she was merely staking her claim for membership of their agency and he liked it. He'd also noticed that the other associates were looking more comfortable and that warmed his heart. Perhaps, after all these years, he was becoming a team player.

'That would be great Bec...Rebecca,' he replied.

'A'm happy tae continue keeping ma ear tae the ground,' said Jake.

'That can't be easy for a man of your stature,' said Callum, having taken an instant a liking to the big man.

'It's easy when you're sitting on your arse most of the time,' replied Jake.

'That must be where I've seen you before, sitting on the bench at the end of the Kirkgate,' said Callum.

'Aye, that's my look-out post.' Jake handed the almost empty bag of savouries to Mark. 'Get tore in

Son.'

'I'll have a hard job, there's hardly a crumb left in there,' said Mark looking into the bag.

'You'd better speak to the Minister about that,' said Jake, 'he must have been gie hungry himself, he had two sausage rolls, and a pie tae boot.'

Tracey returned with the tea and mini-doughnuts, just in time to prevent another Callum soliloquy, or so she thought.

'Then there's Shifty Stewart,' said Callum, warming up again.

'Who's he, when he's at home?' asked Mark.

'He's not at home, at least not any more,' said Callum. 'He's dead.

'I think I've heard of him, said Tracey.

'William, alias Shifty Stewart's body was found after he'd escaped from prison in the south of England, but he hailed from Leith,' explained Callum.

'And?' asked Tod, interested but dreading the start of another monologue.

'He owned dozens of properties, drove luxury cars and had millions stashed away in bank accounts around the globe. The known drug baron had been on the run since his escape from prison and was thought to have fled abroad, but it turned out he was in Britain and he died penniless in London.'

'Excuse me for asking,' asked Rebecca, 'but what has this to do with our case?'

'There remain doubts about why Mr Stewart, a Category A high-risk prisoner, described as one of Scotland's most dangerous men, was transferred to an open prison in Dorset. Of course, it was easy for him to escape from there.'

'Why are you so interested in this Stewart character?' asked Mark, 'and why should we be?'

'Our William was caught at sea, handling a very large quantity of Class A drugs and a customs official was killed during the police raid. He really did have a finger in every pie and he would have known of any illegal imports coming into Leith.'

Rebecca coughed at the mention of fingers and pies. 'But you've just told us he's dead.'

'Aye but his best friend isn't, is he Tracey,' said Callum.

'No,' answered Tracey.

'Shifty was never one to shy away from friendships, especially those that made for lucrative business deals and whilst in prison who did he befriend, but Jimmy

McGuire. The two were inseparable in fact, until of course Shifty was transferred.'

'How did he manage that?' asked Mark.

'He claimed the move was necessary so that he could be near his estranged wife in Dorset. Now there are unsubstantiated claims that MI5 agents helped Stewart's move and disappearance and that he may have been murdered to prevent the full extent of his links to the security services emerging. His body was found in March 2004, but it took a month for the authorities to reveal that information. A Westminster spokeswoman said there were many unanswered questions surrounding the case.'

'How do you know that Stewart and Jimmy McGuire were talking about business?' asked Tracey. 'Jimmy may have been trying to convert the drug dealer.'

Callum ignored Tracey's comment, and no one could tell from his face what he was thinking.

'Was the drugs' haul here, in Leith?' asked Tod.

'No, it was off the north coast in September 1995. Stewart was sentenced to twenty-five years in prison for it. A year later this was reduced to eighteen years when the Court of Appeal ruled that the judge had been punishing Stewart for the death of the customs man, even though he had not been charged in connection with it. Five years into his sentence, Stewart was transferred to several different prisons until he was in one known for its relaxed regime and high number of absconders. It was designed to help inmates readjust to the outside world and town visits were common. Despite Stewart's standing in the criminal underworld and the fact that he had access to vast wealth and strong contacts abroad, the police treated his escape as low priority. A worldwide alert was not put out until the end of March. Four days after that, he was found dead.'

'A'll speak tae him about this,' said Tracey.

'A ken ye've found God but are you in touch wie the dead now?' asked Jake.

'Not Stewart, stupid, Jimmy McGuire! A'll speak tae Jimmy McGuire.'

CHAPTER SIX

Tuesday 11th November

'Sandra, I've told you twice already,' shouted Bob, 'I have looked everywhere, even under the bloody desks, and I can't find any information relating to the death of William Stewart in 2004, other than what I can glean from the public search engines. Every time I enter his name into our records or speak with anyone in authority it's the same old story – **RESTRICED ACCESS!**'

'Uncle Peter, I'm sorry I've not been in touch, I've been somewhat busy of late.' Rebecca had summoned-up the courage to phone her uncle for the first time since the revelations, about his involvement in the Fort House Case, hit the newspapers.

'Too busy to phone your uncle, Beccy.'

'I am sorry, I...'

'Please don't apologise. I'm not surprised that you didn't phone. Though it does amaze me just how many of my friends, and family, have done the same. I think the term is ostracised by association.'

'You do know those revelations were nothing to do with me, or JP Associates, don't you Uncle Peter?'

'I do know that you had nothing to do with this

Rebecca, but I think it would be better if we left it at that.'

'Oh, Uncle Peter, it could have been anyone. What makes you think it was Bobby?'

'Something I said to him when you visited my club last time you were in London. I gave him some advice that, in hindsight, I should have kept to myself.'

Rebecca thought for a moment. 'That wouldn't be when you called him back into the club as we were about to leave? I thought you were just trying to twist his arm to have another drink.'

'I was only trying to help. Anyway, why the phone call now?'

'Have you heard of a William Stewart?'

There was silence on the other end of the phone, which told Rebecca her uncle had indeed heard of him. 'Are you still there, Uncle Peter?'

When he eventually spoke it was in a tone of voice that Rebecca had never heard. *'What has that bloody copper got you involved in now?'*

'Would that be a yes then, Uncle?'

'Please give me Bob's new phone-number, I want a word with him.'

'You know I can't do that, and anyway this has nothing to do with Bob.'

'I don't believe that for one moment Rebecca. If it's not Bob, it's that organisation of his, the one you've got yourself entangled with. If it's not Bob James then it's his partner, Tod Peterson.'

'You seem to know a lot about our agency Uncle. How can that be? I haven't told you about it.'

'Rebecca, please do not get involved in anything to do with William Stewart. You must promise me that, please!'

'What have you heard about him? We believe that the Security Services may have been involved in some way in his escape from prison and his subsequent death.

'Rebecca, please just do as I ask. Will you do that for me?'

'I was hoping you could help me. I've been through, and am still going through, a lot and I wanted to show the agency that I am more than a mere fund manager. It helps take my mind off Richard and Sophie, that's all.'

Peter had forgotten momentarily the plight his niece was in. *'Rebecca, I am so sorry. I do worry about you darling. Please promise me you won't ask any more questions regarding William Stewart, and that includes putting his name into any search-engine. You must promise me that. If you do, I will make sure that your agency gets the information it needs.'*

Rebecca's promised. When the call was over Uncle Peter opened his desk drawer and took out a mobile phone from a locked compartment. Once he'd made the call, he took his old leather suitcase, the one with the cruise stickers showing where he and his deceased wife Wilhelmina had travelled during their years of marriage. Prior to putting his clothes in the case, he lifted the false bottom and removed the military pistol. Before replacing it, he checked to see if it was loaded. 'It's been a wee while since we've been north of the border,' he said, as he continued packing.

Just as Rebecca's Uncle Peter was warning her off from using the internet to search for information regarding the life and times of Shifty Stewart, Harry Cowan was logging on. Fortunately, Harry had on numerous occasions, learned enough about crime and the workings of GCHQ, never to use his home computer when researching crime or espionage. He was therefore sitting in an internet café when he typed "William Stewart" into the search engine.

Once he'd logged on and begun his search he was surprised he couldn't find very much about Stewart, nothing more than what the Reverend Mackie had told them in the office. What he did discover was that books had been written about the man, and many of them described him as one of the most dangerous men in Scotland. That got Harry to thinking about Tracey and her involvement with Jimmy McGuire. She had always had a soft spot for those less fortunate than herself. Harry thought at times that that was why she'd taken up with him. He'd seen a change though since he'd started learning and had become a community teacher. There was a change in the way she looked at him and the way she addressed him, and it hinted at respect.

He knew that Bob James was absolutely against Tracey visiting McGuire in prison and teaching him English. In Bob's opinion McGuire was a scammer and would use any means possible to get what he wanted, and that usually meant advancement in the criminal fraternity. Bob didn't believe for one minute that McGuire had turned over the new leaf he was brandishing and had become a Christian. Neither did Tod. But Tracey did and all of them knew she was unstoppable once she got the bit between her teeth.

After reading about the exploits of Stewart and how bad he'd been, Harry decided he'd give it one more try and have a word with her.

CHAPTER SEVEN

Wednesday 12th November

'Not on your life, Harry Cowan! That man has changed, and it happened in the jail and I can think of somebody else, not that far fae here, who did the same thing. How would you like it if everybody, including Bob James and Tod Peterson, went around telling all and sundry that Harry Cowan was a fraudster and that he was still a crook? No, you widnae like that, would you Harry!'

Harry was already regretting having raised the subject. He knew she was right about one thing though, he wouldn't like it if he was still seen as a criminal. But that wasn't enough to stop him in his attempt to make her see sense. 'Even Tod doesn't think you visiting McGuire is a good idea, and Tod has taught English tae some of the worst criminals in Edinburgh.'

'For your information, Tod is helping me tae teach Jimmy. He's giving me loads of handouts and talks tae me about it all the time,' replied Tracey.

'He didnae tell me that. Anywie, he's just humouring you. It doesnae mean he believes in McGuire's conversion!'

'Well A do believe in Jimmy McGuire's conversion Harry, just like A believe in yours and I will not stop helping him. When Tod taught me tae read and write it opened a whole world tae me and that's what A'm gonnae dae for Jimmy, and neither you, nor anybody else for that matter, will stop me. Have you got that?'

'Darling, A'm really worried about this Shifty Stewart character and...'

Tracey stopped him in his tracks. 'So, the truth is out. This isnae about Jimmy McGuire, is it? This is all about William Stewart. You're worried about your poor wee wife getting herself involved in something way over her head.'

'What?'

'Dinnae be shy Babe. There's nothing wrong with you being worried about me dealing with all those big bad men in prison, what wie me being a woman and all that.' Tracey stroked his cheek. 'Aw didums, you were just worried about me.' She kissed the cheek she'd just stroked.

Harry took a moment to compose himself. 'What time dae you start work?'

'Half-twelve, why? Oh no you don't Harry Cowan, A've some shopping tae dae for the office first.'

It was mid-morning on the same day that Harry was getting the knock-back from Tracey that Jake and Mark sat on the bench at the end of the Kirkgate. Mark had just delivered Jake's coffee from the café where he worked to fund his doctorate in psychology.

'A'm at a bit of a loose end regarding Tod's new conspiracy, tae be honest Mark.' Jake lifted the lid from his cardboard cup.

'To be honest Jake, I'm really not that interested. Come to that, I no longer think I'm needed by JP Associates. I haven't done much for them since the last case. I'm not even sure if I've fallen out of favour with Tod.'

'A thought ye were a psychologist Son? Tod has been looking after you since the death of your pal Karl, that's all. He doesn't want you getting too involved, what wie you needing tae finish the PhD and that. It's just he doesnae ken how tae show his feelings, but A ken he likes you and dinnae you go thinking otherwise.'

'I suppose you're right, but I do feel left out sort of, and if that's how it feels for me, then it's the truth.'

'A psychologist right enough,' said Jake, smiling. He put his hand on the young man's shoulder. 'Anywie, what are we going tae dae about this grand phantom of Tod's?'

'The first thing I'd do would be talk to the sailor who gave Tod the information in the first place. Find out if he is the genuine article or if he's just gone off on one. It does happen you know, especially after all those months and years at sea.'

'Good idea,' said Jake, 'but that would require us taking a rowing boat and rowing half way to Russia. I think gaining access to the man could be more difficult than you think.'

'Maybe the minister could arrange it?' said Mark.

Jake took his hand from Mark's shoulder. 'I think I might just have a wee idea or two where that's concerned, if you're in?'

'I'm in,' said Mark, shivering slightly, 'it's got to be better than being left out in the cold.'

'Well, how did you think it went on Monday?'

'What?' asked Tracey, knowing full well what Tod was referring to.'

'You know fine to what I'm referring, the team meeting.'

'Oh that, I think it went off without a hitch.'

'Do you think they feel as if they are part of the team now?'

'They always did Tod. They were just winding you up when they complained about being left out. I hope you don't mind me saying but maybe you should get out a bit more.'

'Well, O wise one, how are you feelings about the case?'

'What case? Oh, you mean the grand, hooded phantom case. Not much really.'

Before Tod could object, Tracey continued. 'Harry doesn't want me to ask any questions relating to Shifty Stewart.'

'Why?'

'He thinks he was one bad lot and Harry's worried about me.'

'Maybe you should listen to him.'

'And maybe you should mind your own business and let me deal with this in my own way. Chivalry is alive and well and living in Leith eh.'

'That's not fair, and you know it Tracey. I'm merely worried for you, and so is Harry; after all, you've managed to get the ear of someone much worse than Shifty Stewart.'

'Why can't you men get it into your thick heads that people can change, and Jimmy McGuire is one of them! He has changed, okay!'

The two colleagues were silent for a few moments

before Tracey continued. 'Talking about folk changing, Jake and I are a wee bit worried about Mark. He's just not been the same since his friend Karl's death.'

'I agree,' said Tod, still thinking about Jimmy McGuire and his supposed rebirth.

'Get over it boss; Jimmy McGuire is my problem. What about Mark?'

'Do you think that Karl's suicide is the only thing that's bothering him?' asked Tod, breaking free from his reverie.

'To be quite honest with you, no I don't.'

'What is it then, in your opinion?'

'A think he's feeling rejected,'

'What could have caused that?'

'You!'

'Me, what have I done this time?'

'Mark was really helpful tae us on the Jane Keen case but since then he's been given the heave-ho. Aye you took him wie ye on your travels around the New Town on the Fort case and you got him tae enlist Karl tae dae your research, and we know what happened to him. A think that is what's bothering him.'

Tod thought for a moment. 'Didn't you just say that

you thought everyone was okay and that they'd been winding me up about feeling left out?'

'Aye, all except Mark.'

Tod moved over to the plastic wall clock and adjusted the hands. 'This thing has never been right since Harry brought it in.' He sat down at the coffee table. 'You may be right about Mark. My problem now though is that Mark was consulted on the Jane Keen case because we needed someone with knowledge of psychology. I only took him around the New Town with me, during the Fort case, because I wanted to keep an eye on him after the death of his friend Karl. Since then, we have genuinely not needed his services.'

'All A can say tae that is A hope you continue to need mine, if that's what ye dae tae folk when ye dinnae need them! Dae you not think he'll ken that he's been given the bum's rush? He's daen a PhD in psychology Tod, stop treating him like a bairn! And stop calling him "Son" for that matter; it gets on ma nerves and probably his as well!'

Tod stood and strode into the kitchen. Tracey could hear him filling the kettle and smiled to herself, knowing full well her boss would be on the phone to Mark as soon as she was out of earshot.

'Sorry boss,' she said, as Tod reappeared with two cups of coffee, 'but you needed to hear that.'

'Maybe you're right.'

The lack of a suitable response from Tod caused Tracey to change the subject 'Have you seen much of Valerie lately?'

'No.'

'She popped in yesterday hoping to see you, but you weren't around.'

'She what?'

'We had a good blether, and A was telling her all about the grand, hooded phantom. She's a right nice lassie that. Just your cup of tea, A'd say, though maybe a wee bit young for you.'

'I'd rather not talk about Valerie, Tracey.'

'There you go again! First it's Mark and now Valerie. Have you no use for her either now that the Fort case is done and dusted?'

'She is not part of the team, that's all.'

'Have you been missing her?'

Tod shrugged. 'I've not heard from Valerie since her exhibition at the Scottish Parliament. Immediately after that she was taken on as an Arts Inclusion worker for the government and has been all over Scotland. I think she maybe thought that Mark and I were using her exhibition for our own ends.'

'You were! And I'd forgotten about Mark helping you there. Anywie, after Valerie and I had our blether she had a wee look round the office and asked if we'd like one of her paintings tae hang on the wall; she said that our picture of two dolphins diving through surf is not in vogue.'

'What did you say?'

'A said I'm quite happy wie the dolphins: they remind me of you and Bob.'

'You what! Tracey I...'

'A'm only kidding. She's popping in with it at three, that's in about half an hour. A'll be heading off then of course so you'll need tae look after her.'

As promised Valerie did arrive at three. She was carrying a large brown-paper parcel which Tod took to be the painting. He was about to utter the same when Valerie put her finger to her lips, gesturing silence. 'Missed you,' she said.

Tod's faced flushed. 'Missed you too.' He walked up to her and removed the painting from her arms. 'It looks heavy.'

'In more ways than one,' she replied. 'You'll need a

strong hook and a stronger constitution for this one, Arts man.'

'How's the new job?' asked Tod, ignoring her reference to his Arts degree.

'Good. Very good, in fact. They've even given me transport. It seems I've landed, at last.'

'Joined the establishment I think it's called,' said Tod.

'You should know all about joining the establishment with your Community Education background.'

'Wordsworth did something like you. Radical as a poet, reactionary later; he became a tax collector for the government in the end.'

'I'm teaching isolated communities how to use art to express their real lives, for good and bad.'

'I'm sure it's worthwhile.'

'The plan is that once they are accustomed to using art as a medium, then I present them with their tax demands.' Valerie was one of the few people, other than Bob James and Tracey, who could catch Tod off guard and make him laugh spontaneously. 'Well are you going to ask me out or not?'

'Not sure, I've never been out with a tax collector,' replied Tod.

CHAPTER EIGHT

Thursday 13th November

When Tracey opened the office at twelve-thirty the next day she noticed the still wrapped painting lying against the wall. There had obviously been no time for art appreciation, she thought as she began unwrapping the work. As she did so she pondered on why she felt such a strong instinct to mother Tod. She knew he was capable of looking after himself, yet she often detected that there existed a very vulnerable side to him. He never discussed his past, his family or his feelings and it seemed to her at times that her boss carried the weight of the world on his shoulders. Each time she'd tried to get him to talk about it, he'd just brush it off with a standard Scottish male reply, "I'm fine."

Once she'd put the wrapping in the waste-basket Tracey stood back to view the picture. She recognised Newhaven Harbour immediately. The sun was setting over the sea wall and small pleasure craft and one solitary lobster boat lay on the still water within the old fishing harbour. In the distance two oil rigs were silhouetted against the Fife hills and although in the background, they cast their shadows across the pier. Tracey was studying the work closely when the office door opened.

'We'll need to put a stronger hook in the wall to hold that,' said Tod.

'Aye, definitely,' said Tracey. 'She's not much of an artist, is she? She's got the sunset all wrong, it sinks in the west, over the Forth Bridge, not over the hills of Fife. Those rigs couldnae cast a shadow from where they are.'

Tod looked at the painting. 'That's what I was telling you, remember, her work is almost allegorical and certainly subjective. I think it's her way of pointing out that oil put paid to traditional Scottish industry, like fishing, and she is using artistic license to achieve her aim.'

'Aye, well it's too clever for me. How did ye get on last night?'

'Last night?'

'Aye, wie Valerie. A'm assuming you took her for her tea.'

'Actually, we did go for something to eat.'

'Is that it? Am A not getting the nitty-gritty? Oh, and by the way, did you phone Mark?'

'Yes, I did, but...' Tod was interrupted by the door opening.

A tall elderly gentleman in a long dark Crombie overcoat walked straight up to them both and put out his hand to shake Tod's. 'Peter, Peter Blue,' he said, before Valerie's painting caught his eye.

'I'm sorry,' said Tod, 'do I know...' he stopped mid flow.

'That's right, Rebecca's uncle. I arrived this morning. There have been many changes at the airport since I was last here. It was called Turnhouse Airport then and one could park at the terminal without having to take out a mortgage.'

'What can we dae for ye?' asked Tracey, seeing her boss struggle for words.

'That's a fine watercolour. A recent acquisition?' asked Peter.

'Aye,' answered Tracey, much to Tod's annoyance. He wanted this man out of the office.

'Valerie seems to prefer watercolour, does she?' asked Peter.

'It's an allegory,' said Tracey, hoping her newly acquired fine-art language would help stem Tod's rising anger.

'Do you know Valerie's work?' Tod asked.

'No, but her name is scrawled across the bottom of the picture, along with the year date '14, unless of course that is her age,' said Peter, pointing to the signature.

'Listen,' said Tod, moving closer to him, 'what do you

want?'

'I was hoping to see Rebecca, actually. Is she not here?'

'No, she's not here,' replied Tod.

'I've been to her house but there's no sign of her. I've tried her mobile and I've been taking taxis around the city, trying to find her but to no avail. Your cabs are more expensive than in London, I've got to say.'

'Well she's not here,' replied Tod. 'Now, can I ask you to leave, we're rather busy and I don't think we have any other business to discuss, do you.'

'I wouldn't like to think of my niece as mere business, Mr Peterson, if that is what you are implying.'

'Why are you really here Mr Blue? Is this to do with the Fort case? Have the powers that be been up to their old tricks again? You're obviously off the hook; was it a handshake that did it this time, merely a case of greasing a few palms in the old boys' network?'

'Mm, I see you do not think very highly of me or our glorious establishment, for that matter. Perhaps we'll get the chance to discuss the subject in more detail another time Mr Peterson, and in different circumstances.' Peter's veiled threat was not missed by Tod, or by Tracey. 'Anyway, should you come across Rebecca, I would appreciate it if you could tell her that her Uncle Peter is in Edinburgh and would like to treat her to dinner. I believe you have some upmarket restaurants here in Leith.'

Neither Tod nor Tracey answered this last remark, leaving the old man with nothing more to say.

Peter had only just left the office when Tod phoned Bob.

'What do you mean Rebecca's Uncle Peter is here?' Bob shouted down the phone.

'That's what I said, he's only just left the office. He says he's not here about the Fort case, that's been put to bed as far as he is concerned.'

'Aye right, so it has! Does he think we're stupid? No, don't answer that.'

'What do you want me to do?' asked Tod.

'Do? Do nothing, at least until I've spoken to Beccy.'

Bob hung up on Tod and immediately texted Rebecca, but there was no reply.

For a man who'd not been in Edinburgh for many years, Uncle Peter certainly knew his way around Leith. Turning right into Henderson Street he was soon at the doors of South Leith Parish Church Halls. When he entered, he found himself in the queue for the foodbank. Immediately he saw who he'd come looking for and decided to wait to be served. He kept his head down until he reached the serving table.

Callum was busy lifting bags of non-perishable foodstuff onto the table for those who had the job of handing them out to the waiting clients. At first he didn't see the well-dressed gentleman. Sadie Mairns, one of the volunteers, took one look at the gentleman and immediately assumed, wrongly as it turned out, he'd come to the wrong place.

'I'm sorry, but this is a foodbank,' was all she could think to say.'

'Yes.' replied Peter. 'Actually, I'm here to see this gentleman.' He pointed at Callum.

When Callum looked up he almost fell backwards. 'Sir, I thought you said on the phone you were only thinking of coming up.'

'I did Callum. Anyway, no need for pleasantries, Sergeant Mackie,' replied Peter, much to the surprise of the lady handing out the food-bags. 'Perhaps I could have a moment of your time.' It wasn't a question.

Callum made his apologies to the other volunteers and the two men left the church halls and headed to the far corner of the car-park.

'Remind me again, to what do I owe this pleasure Colonel?'

'As I said on the phone, I was thinking of coming up for a visit, and here I am; I only arrived this morning.'

'And you thought you'd look me up straight away. Who told you I'd be at the foodbank?'

Peter tapped the side of his nose but didn't answer.

'Not that little bird again, I should have guessed.'

'How are you getting on in your new profession Callum?'

'As you well know, I've retired from the ministry.'

'It didn't look like that to me.' He pointed back to the halls. 'There are some unfortunate individuals in there, are there not.'

'What is it you want, Sir?'

'Do you remember the job we did together all those years ago, more than a distant memory now I imagine?'

'Oh aye, I remember that job, Sir.'

'You see, unlike your present employ Callum, in our line of work one can never really retire.'

'Tell me, what would the service want with an old man like me, Sir?'

'It's not so much the service Callum, as me. My niece Rebecca has got mixed up with a shady bunch of characters here in Leith and I would really appreciate it if you could keep an eye on her for me.'

'What shady bunch might that be Sir?'

'They call themselves JP Associates and have an office round in Great Junction Street, by the bus-stop. They are a sort of investigation agency and my niece is helping fund their little venture. You've maybe heard of them?'

Callum nearly choked when he realised that he'd been sitting with the niece of retired Colonel and MI5 director Peter Blue only a few days before in the said JP Associates.

'Leith is a small place and I have heard of them. They've not been here very long, I believe.'

'Long enough to make an impact in high places. But we digress, that is not why I'm here. JP Associates has got itself caught up in the William Stewart scandal. You'll remember that story Callum. Weren't you asked to look after the Edinburgh side of things back then? Anyway, when Rebecca asked me about Stewart over the phone, it wasn't too difficult for me to put two and two together and that's why I've come to Edinburgh. I don't think she has any idea what she has involved herself in.'

'Mm,' answered Callum, not wanting to give away that he too was involved.

'So, will you do a favour for an old friend and keep an eye on her?'

Callum moved closer to his ex-colonel. 'I'll do as ordered Sir. But Sir, please never use my military title in public again.' He looked Peter directly in the eyes.

'That's my man,' said Peter, completely unfazed by the threat in Callum's request. 'I knew you wouldn't let me down.'

CHAPTER NINE

Friday 14th November

Callum Mackie knew that Tod and Bob were to be found in the Starbank Inn most Friday evenings after work. When he arrived, he saw that the two men had found the most deserted part of the bar-room, a difficult task indeed on a Friday at six o'clock, with both locals and office staff carrying a week-long drouth and vying for service.

The two investigators were deep in conversation, leaning on the bar, elbows touching. Each had a whisky in hand. Callum ordered three doubles and asked the barman to take two of them over to Tod and Bob. When the barman put the drinks in front of them, both turned instantly to look for their benefactor. Neither could believe their eyes when they saw it was Callum Mackie; until then he'd never put his hand in his pocket. They knew by instinct it must be serious, whatever it was, to have caused such a change. Bob beckoned him over.

'I didn't want to disturb you,' said Callum as he approached.

'That's okay,' said Bob, 'we were only having a blether.'

'I could see that,' replied Callum, 'a very intimate blether from the way you were huddled up.'

'Cheers,' said Tod, picking up his whisky glass and resisting the temptation to mention "no such thing as a free lunch".

'I wanted a word, if you don't mind?' said Callum, clinking glasses with the two men.

'Go for it,' said Tod.

'Out with it,' said Bob, almost simultaneously.

'You two certainly make a good double act,' replied Callum. 'Unfortunately, not everybody is of the same opinion as me.'

'And who might they be?' asked Bob.

'I've heard you described recently as a mere toy-town investigation agency.' Callum smiled.

'Now, I think I know who may have implied that,' said Tod. 'His name doesn't happen to be Jake Robinson, by any chance?'

'That's a good guess, I'll give you that. Unfortunately, it is someone much higher up the pecking order than Jake.'

'Right, enough of the mystery Callum. We've a lot on our plate without you throwing in any more spanners,' said Bob.

'You'll have both heard of Colonel Peter Blue, no

doubt.'

'Uncle Peter?' queried Tod, turning to look at Bob.

'The very one, and the very reason I am here. Uncle Peter,' he too looked at Bob, 'is here in Edinburgh because his darling niece has got herself mixed up with some "toy-town investigation agency" and he'd like me to keep an eye on her.'

'What's really going on here Callum? I didn't even know that you knew Peter Blue.'

'That's by the by Bob, but he is on a mission.'

'What mission?' interrupted Tod.

'I've told you, to serve and protect his darling Rebecca. He believes she has got herself involved with you and by default is involved in an investigation into the goings-on of a certain William Stewart. Peter Blue certainly does not want that to happen. Apart from the obvious dangers surrounding William Stewart, dead or not, there is the possible involvement of MI5 in his death and disappearance, and that allegedly happened when Uncle Peter was in charge. So, you could say there is a little self-interest at the heart of Peter looking after darling Rebecca.'

Bob didn't like it when Rebecca's name was mentioned, and he always felt defensive, especially when the prefix "darling" was attached to her name. He knew that most of his associates in JP thought of her as his "posh tottie". 'Has he met with Rebecca since he arrived?'

'No, she's not to be found.'

'If you don't mind me repeating Bob's question Callum, how do you know Peter Blue?' asked Tod.

'I do mind you asking, actually. We have a shared past and that's all I'm telling you, for the moment.'

'Special Forces?' asked Bob.

'Something like that,' answered Callum. 'How did you guess? No, don't bother to answer that. What I can tell you about Peter Blue is that behind his gentlemanly exterior lies a very cold heart. He is a ruthless and dangerous man, and he is not one to cross. Anyone hurting, or even threatening Rebecca's safety would soon know about it.'

'That sounds almost like a threat Callum,' said Bob. 'I hope it's not directed at me?'

'Why would that be a threat to you Bob?' asked Callum.

Bob ignored the question. 'Does Peter know know us?'

'Absolutely not. Why do you think I've been ordered to keep an eye out for Rebecca and report back?'

'Ordered? Does Colonel Blue still have a hold over you then?' asked Tod.

Callum took a large quaff of his whisky. 'Let's just say we've a history that ties us together. Anyway, I suppose the bottom line is that when a man doesn't have much more to do than tend his pelargoniums, any new venture is a welcome change. Keeping an eye out for Rebecca is hardly going to cause me sleepless nights,' he looked from one to the other, 'or is it?'

At the mention of sleepless nights, Tod cringed. He knew what these were. 'You tell us. You were the one who introduced the subject of Shifty Stewart in the first place.'

'Excuse me for interrupting,' interrupted Bob, 'but what I don't understand is Uncle Peter's sudden interest in JP Associates? What if Bec...Rebecca did mention William Stewart, he's bloody dead. It's hardly worth her uncle coming to Edinburgh to protect her from a dead body, is it?'

'We all know that JP Associates seem to have a knack of turning mere conspiracy into fact, much to Peter's discredit, as far as I'm aware. My guess is he is not only worried about Rebecca mentioning William Stewart but by the fact that as she is working with you. That would be enough to set Peter's alarm bells ringing, don't you think Bob? Uncle Peter probably believes you are on to something dangerous, and his niece is involved.' Callum took another sip of his whisky.

'Aye, and you said you weren't involved in Tod's conspiracy theory,' said Bob. 'Pull the other one, it's got bells on.'

They laughed simultaneously at Bob's analogy, encouraging him to lean on the bar and order three more whiskies.

'This is for your ears only,' said Bob raising his glass to toast his friends. 'Believe me, this is pure coincidence, but at moment the Cold Case Squad is revisiting Stewart's prison escape, his disappearance and subsequent death.'

'Now that is what I call a coincidence and thank you for sharing it with us, Inspector,' said Tod. 'Does this mean JP Associates is doing the work for DI Sandra Laing and her Squad? After all, you know what Tracey, and Einstein said about coincidences.'

'Now don't get all hot under the collar Tod. I am one of you, remember. I have to be very careful because of the "conflict of interest", which I'm still reminded of on a daily basis. Although I am only a consultant with Police Scotland, I remain within the parameters of its rules and regulations. And I can assure you, this is pure coincidence. The fact that Stewart's name came up at your meeting has nothing to do with me.' He looked at Callum. 'But now that it has come up, there might just be some scope for joint working.'

'So, they have reopened the case,' said Callum. 'It's about time.'

'Something like that,' replied Bob, 'Except all gates are closed for the moment.'

'Well that is confirmation, if I've ever heard it. JP Associates are about to do Police Scotland's work for them again.' Tod, looked directly at Bob. 'Well at least we are off to a head start as Tracey has organised a visit to McGuire to discuss his relationship with Stewart whilst both were in Edinburgh Prison.'

It was as well Bob wasn't taking a sip of his drink at that moment or he may have choked. He went red in the face. 'What!'

'No point in trying to put her off Bob, you should know that,' smiled Tod. 'And it may just get us the information we need.'

'I think that calls for another drink, don't you Tod,' suggested Callum, before Bob could get a word in. Callum then indicated it was Tod's turn to buy.

Just as Tod was about to call the barman over, he was interrupted by a loud voice. 'Make mine a double Grouse!' The three men turned as one to see a well-built, elderly man smiling at them. Though he seemed to be well over sixty years of age, he stood straight-backed and looked as hard as nails.

'Well if it isn't our Sandy Grassick,' said Callum, putting his hand on the man's shoulder. 'Shouldn't you be out there on the Forth laying your creels?'

'Done and dusted and I've a drouth that would choke a camel. Dead of winter, Minister, a man likes to get back in from the darkness; especially if there's a free dram waiting for him.' This left Tod thinking, not another one.

Sandy looked at Tod, as if reading his mind, before turning back to Callum. 'Have you put your hand in that deep pocket of yours Minister?'

'I was just about to get them in but this gentleman here,' Callum pointed at Tod, 'insisted.'

'Aye right,' said Sandy. 'Have I caught you in mid-flow with one of your seafaring tales?'

'It was nothing but a wee story about the oil game and the flotsam and jetsam that finds its way into our beautiful port of Leith. These men believe that there is more to those oil supply ships than meets the eye. Something that puts our beloved port to shame, and they have the port authorities in their sight.'

'Interesting. And what exactly would it be that's finding its way to our shores?'

'Bayani, a Filipino sailor from the coal boat, has got them thinking that Leith just might be the destination for illicit cargo and those "monsters of the deep", as he calls the oils-rig supply ships, might be the vehicles.'

'Well I never, and right under our noses. Here's me wasting my time at the lobsters when I could have made a fine packet elsewhere.'

Callum went on to introduce Sandy to Tod and Bob before either could object to his description of their conversation. He described Sandy as an old friend and as they shook hands, explained that he'd fished the Forth, man and boy and still worked his old lobster boat out of Newhaven Harbour.

'Are you still making a living Sandy?' asked Callum.

'Aye, the auld Selich is still looking after me.'

'Is that your boat?' asked Tod, but he was ignored.

'That's good to know. You're certainly looking fit. What age are you now?'

'I'll be seventy-two come December. What about yourself Callum, have you retired yet?'

'Shepherds don't retire Sandy, as well you know.'

'Neither do sailors, as far as I ken. It's been a wee while since I've been in your kirk.'

'Fifteen years and three months to the day,' said Callum.

'You remember then? You always did have a good memory.'

'Oh aye, I remember. And you wouldn't answer your door to me when I came visiting after you left.'

Bob and Tod looked on and listened as the two old friends came to terms with Sandy's absence from church. Then Callum expanded the story which the Filipino sailor had told Tod and how they were all flummoxed by it.

'You shouldnae believe everything you hear from sailors,' replied Sandy, with a smile. After being offered another drink by Bob, Sandy gave his apologies. When Callum repeated the offer of another dram, much to the surprise of his friends, Sandy refused again, on the grounds he had to get home to feed his cat.

After Sandy had left the pub, Bob was the first to enquire. 'Auld Selich is looking after him?'

'I think I've worked that one out,' said Tod. 'It's the old Scots word for the Silkie, am I right?'

'Aye, and it's not the name of his boat; he named that after his wife Maggie. Sandy took to the old mythology big time when she died. They were inseparable, except when he was at sea of course. Now he believes her spirit is with him in the shape of a seal. When he is out on the Forth he is back with his lovely Maggie and when he is at home he just keeps himself to himself, but my guess is it was her he was going home to just now. He's never had a cat as long as I've known him.'

'Jesus Christ,' said Bob, immediately regretting it. 'Sorry I...'

'No need to apologise for bringing up our Lord's name Bob. He'll be delighted to join us. Sandy was a staunch believer but gave up believing when Maggie died. She developed breast cancer and didn't last long. That was the last the kirk saw of him, fifteen years and three months ago.'

'That is some memory you've got there Callum,' said Bob. 'How do you remember such detail when you must have had a great many parishioners on your watch?'

'Oh, I'll never forget Sandy. As a boy, he was on the last whaling ship from Leith to South Georgia and knew it well. Later, he became an expert inshore fisherman so when the Falklands War started, he offered up his services as a volunteer to the navy, and they jumped at the offer.'

'Were you there?' asked Tod.

Callum ignored the question. 'He was some character. He had the ratings in hoots of laughter with his jokes and stories from his past. And when it came to getting them on shore in our landing boats there was no-one better qualified. He truly is a master of the sea, but it was tragic when he lost Maggie. She'd been complaining to their GP about a pain in her chest and had been treated with antibiotics and painkillers, without being sent for an X-ray. When she was eventually sent, it was far too late to treat her cancer. She only survived two weeks after that. The story is that Sandy went to have a word with her GP, but that's all rumour. Nobody really knows what happened except that the doctor retired early, and Sandy went off the radar.'

'I wouldn't like to cross him,' said Bob. 'He looks as strong as an ox.'

'He is a strong man our Sandy and he has his Selich on his side too.'

'I didn't think a Church of Scotland minister would believe in such stuff.' commented Tod.

'It would amaze you what we Ministers believe Tod, but for the most part we believe in what helps people get through the pain of living, as long as they're not doing harm. Sandy and his Selich are not doing anyone any harm, and doing him some good, of that you can be assured. Now, whose turn is it to get them in?'

CHAPTER TEN

Monday 17ᵗʰ November

The weekend passed uneventfully, or so Tod thought. He'd decided to lay off the drink for the rest of the weekend and stay at home. Bob had kept himself busy by visiting Edinburgh's Botanical Gardens, on both Saturday and Sunday. He liked this time of year, when the summer tourist had gone, and the Christmas crowd had yet to arrive. The autumn colour had all but vanished, but he managed to entertain himself by dreaming of the snowdrops to come and by studying the many varieties of trees and shrubs, now bare but showing their brown skeletons. Not many people do that he'd thought, no, they prefer their skeletons well out of sight.

Tod was already in the office when Tracey arrived at lunchtime. He could see immediately that something was wrong, and he assumed Harry had been up to his old tricks at the weekend. He wasn't far wrong.

'The kettle's not long off the boil,' he said, trying to lighten her load.

She took off her coat and hung it on the stand but didn't answer.

He tried again. 'About the sea-monster theory

Tracey, we've decided to call it a day. Bob and I had a chat about it on Friday night. Callum was there too and we all agreed we are wasting our time thinking we can get anywhere by investigating the importing of illegal substances into Leith. It's too much of a long shot. I blame myself really; I should never have listened to that seaman in the first place, but I'd had a few too many. You know what it's like.'

'No, maybe you shouldn't have,' said Tracey, still with her back to him.

Tod had noticed recently that when Tracey was upset with him she adopted Standard English as her language of choice. He'd been unable to work this out and it still baffled him.

'You don't have to be like that with me Tracey. What's up? Is it Harry?'

'Oh yes, it's Harry alright.'

'What's he been up to this time?'

'He was doing alright until he took up with you and this investigation agency!'

'I don't understand. What has he done?'

'He's only gone and burgled the port authority offices last night and got himself arrested, that's all; and all because of your stupid theory about sea-monsters.' She began to cry. 'Harry was doing just fine until he got himself involved with you. Now he's back in jail, and it's your fault, entirely!' She turned round to face him.

'I don't understand, I never asked Harry to break into any offices.'

'No, but you know what he's like. He thought he was doing you a favour, like he thinks you're doing me one by giving me a job. He's still trying to make that up to you!'

'Where is he now?'

'The Leith Police have got him in Constitution Street. He's due in court tomorrow.'

'Oh.' Tod immediately gave his apologies and left the office. He walked to the corner of Henderson Street, took out his mobile and phoned Bob, at the wrong time. Bob was at that moment on the receiving end of another lecture from DI Sandra Laing about the improprieties of interest conflicts. He saw from the screen it was Tod on the phone but answered regardless. '*Bob James.*'

'Bob, it's Tod, we need to speak. Harry's been arrested. He's in Constitution Street Police Station and is going to court tomorrow.'

Bob already knew about Harry's incarceration as it was the subject of his discussion with his DI. '*I'm sorry but I'm busy right now. Who did you say was calling?*'

Tod realised his friend was in a compromising position, most likely with his DI. 'Get to Leith ASAP. I'll be waiting for you in Costa. And Bob, I mean ASAP!'

After explaining to Sandra about the wrong-number and being accused of lying as well as having conflicting interests, Bob gave his apologies and made his way to Costa.

'Now calm down,' said Tod. 'As far as I'm aware he broke into the offices to try to get us information on the oil-rig supply ships.'

'Oh, is that all. That's alright then. How in heaven's name have we got ourselves involved with such a bloody motley crew of misfits and criminals? This is supposed to be a partnership between you and me, not half of Leith!' Bob realised immediately that he'd spoken too loudly, when most of the customers turned to look his way.

'You can forget the lectures Bob. Maybe we need to concentrate on how we are going to get Harry out of this mess. You can complain all you like about me employing Tracey, but remember, it was your idea to get Rebecca on-board, without an interview, and look where that's got us; bloody Uncle Peter! Couldn't you use your influence with Police Scotland?

'Aye right,' replied Bob, 'I'll just wander into the polis

station, show my defunct warrant card and tell them I'd like them to release Harry into my custody. That should work.'

'Don't be funny. I thought maybe you could still pull some strings.'

'Maybe once upon a time Tod, but not anymore.'

Before the conversation could proceed further, the small sinewy figure of Harry Cowan walked up to them and sat down. 'Hi,' he said.

After their third double-take Bob was first to speak. 'What are you doing here? I thought you were banged-up in Constitution Street nick?'

'A was. A was due in court tomorrow but then a tall, posh Englishman showed up and told them that A'm working for him. They brought me fae the cells, and A've got tae be honest, A've never seen him before in my life. But A've never seen so many polis change colour so quickly, when he showed them his ID. Then he walked me out the door and told me you two were waiting for me here. And he told me tae tell you Bob, Rebecca is asking for ye.'

A long silence descended upon the two investigators.

'Are ye no gonnae buy me a coffee?' asked Harry.'

He remained unaware that at that moment he was in great danger of getting more than a coffee. Bob's face turned a bright pink and he was about to say something when Tod beat him to it. 'Harry, what in heaven's name possessed you to break into the offices of the port authorities?'

'You,' answered Harry.

'Me! Me! I never asked you to do that.'

'No, but A knew ye really needed somebody tae have a wee look intae their affairs.'

'Harry, I wanted no such thing and you know it. At the meeting we had in the office, I was only trying to keep you all in the loop, after the slagging I took for not involving you enough last time. I had absolutely no intention of having you break into those offices.'

'How did you get caught?' asked Bob.

'Two jokers leaving the casino at three in the morning saw my torchlight and decided tae look in the windae. A got the fright of ma life and stumbled on tae the alarm. A managed tae get out but the polis caught me at the dock gate. A hadnae taken anything fae the offices so they couldnae dae me wie stealing, but those two witnesses said they'd seen me in the building.'

'Harry,' said Bob, rubbing his weary eyes, 'you are such a fucking idiot. Don't you realise we are all in the shite now?'

'That bloke at the nick said tae tell you you've not tae

worry, Uncle Peter will take care of it.' said Harry.

The third silence of the afternoon descended on the trio. If Bob had been honest he would have admitted that he was inwardly delighted that Rebecca was involved, in some way. But that was inwardly. Outwardly he was about to burst. Harry, never slow on the uptake, took his cue and decided the best option was to leave, sharpish. As he stood up, Tod spoke. 'Did you find anything Harry?'

'Aye this.' He produced a memory stick from his sock. 'The docks are not Scottish. They're owned by a multinational finance company.'

'Surprise, surprise,' said Tod.

'So, what's new,' commented Bob.

After Harry had left the café, Bob and Tod took out their mobile phones and noted down the numbers of their most important contacts. 'Someone knows our every move and I think I know who that might be,' said Bob, as they walked outside and across the road to the waterfront. Both men looked at the swirling tide for a few moments. 'This is where it all began Bob, remember. Any regrets about asking me to join you in your wee adventure?'

'Only occasionally,' answered Bob, smiling. 'Remember when we were nippers, we used to skim the stones on the Forth down at Granton Beach.'

'I do that, and if memory serves me well, I always won.'

'Not this time you won't,' said Bob pulling his arm back and skimming his mobile as far as the rippling water would allow. 'That was ten.'

Tod followed suit and counted the times his phone touched the water before sinking to the muddy bottom. 'I counted twelve,' he said.

'I knew I should have bought a better phone,' laughed Bob.

Once the two men had purchased their new pay-as-you-go, untraceable phones, Bob used its limited battery power to phone Rebecca. After many rings she answered. *'Yes, who is this?'*

Bob realised immediately she would not recognise the number of his new phone.

'It's Bob, don't hang up, please Beccy.'

'Why would I do that?'

'You know why. That stuff with your uncle after the Fort case.'

'Now please don't tell me that was nothing to do with you Bobby. Anyway, Uncle Peter has forgotten about

that. In fact, he says he might have done exactly the same thing, if he had been in your position. I think it's put you up in his estimation, if you must know.

'I suppose he has more to concern himself with now. Can we meet Beccy? I don't have much power left on this phone.'

'What do you mean, "concern himself with now." Is this a business or pleasure call Bob James?'

'I'll take the second option, if you don't mind.'

'In that case, you'd better come to the house, I'm here now. Oh, and Bob don't come by the direct route, there are spies everywhere, and one can't be too careful.'

Tod waited till he was back in the office before phoning Callum. Tracey had gone by the time he'd got there but had left him a note telling him of Harry's release, without charge.

'Callum, it's Tod here.'

'Tod, what can I do for you?'

'Did you manage to get in touch with Rebecca?'

'No, not yet; she's a hard woman to find. Uncle Peter won't be too chuffed.'

'Not anymore he'll not. She was with her uncle this afternoon. I think you can relax about looking for her and as for looking after her, it looks as if her Uncle Peter is more than capable of that himself.'

'Aye, I told you we're not dealing with just any old spook here.'

'Fancy a dram Callum?'

They chose the Starbank Inn for their dram as it was only two hundred yards down the steep hill from Callum's semi-detached, nineteen-thirties villa. Their choice of venue meant Tod could get the number 7 bus directly from the office, leaving him only a short walk by the sea wall to the pub.

While on the bus, Tod was thinking about Callum and how he'd grown to like the man. It was unusual for him to enjoy the company of other people, most attempts to befriend Tod usually resulted in disappointment for those people. In fact, the only friend he did have was Bob James and he'd always been happy to keep it that way. Valerie of course was a different story; he liked to think that she was more than a friend, or at least had the potential to be.

When he'd first met Callum, he'd got the impression that the minister might be slightly unhinged. Since then he'd changed his mind considerably and had decided that what lay beneath the devil bashing minister was a very astute and a very caring man, especially when it came to the under-dog. Tod suspected that Callum's manuscript on sailors was more than a mere history of sea-faring in Leith and much more likely to be a hard-hitting attempt at making change for the least fortunate. That in itself might mean that the two men shared a common goal.

During their evening together in the Starbank Inn, Callum confessed about his time in the Special Boat Service and some of his work with the security services. He also gave Tod information about Uncle Peter, with whom he'd worked in different parts of the globe, including Colombia in the war against the drug cartels. It was what Callum witnessed there that became his driving force when he left the service. He'd seen priests working with Popular Education movements to try to make a difference in the lives of the poor, while other people continued ripping them off for all they could get. His experiences there convinced him that when he returned to civvies, he'd sign up at the University of Edinburgh's New College and become a minister.

The mention of Popular Education movements, a subject close to Tod's heart during his Community Education studies, caused him open up more than usual that night. He told Callum of his working-class background, his time at Cambridge University where he gained Ist class honours in English. His guilt complex reared its head more than once when he discussed the financial struggles that his "Ist" had brought upon his widowed mother, who'd only managed to cope by taking a very early morning cleaning job in a local bakery.

He spoke at length about his failed marriage to the bright, and rich, young thing from the Home Counties and his experience of life amongst the wealthy when he and Barbara had set up home, thanks to Barbara's parents, who'd kindly given them a small cottage in their grounds.

Although Callum was prone to talk at length, he was also a good listener, one who didn't interrupt with an anecdote of his own each time Tod spoke. Callum's only interruption to Tod's tales of woe merely came with a whispered "sorry to hear that". The Minister was such a good listener that at one-point Tod was tempted to divulge his biggest secret, but not quite.

Personal histories out of the way, Tod raised the subject of the grand, hooded phantom but showed little enthusiasm for following up on the case. This led Callum to think that Tod had lost interest.

But then Tod continued. 'Did you know that the port authority is not the local success story we thought it to be?'

'You're talking about International Engineering

Partners, aren't you? They bought the port authority out just after the millennium. They are fund managers and have a massive property, and business portfolio,' answered Callum.

'So, what exactly would a finance company know about shipping?'

'It is a private equity company and consists of equity securities and debt in operating companies. It is a category of investor that has its own set of goals, preferences and investment strategies. They provide working capital to a target company to nurture expansion, new-product development, or restructuring of the company's operations, management, or ownership.'

'So, correct me if I'm wrong, but are telling me the new company knows nothing about shipping?'

'You've got that in one. The nature of the business is it knows about capital. The existing management of the companies that are bought-out usually remain in place to run the day to day work; hence the port authority's continued existence. Did Harry find out anything else when he stumbled into their offices?'

'Aw for Goodness sake Callum, do you know as well?'

'I have friends in high places.' Callum pointed to the ceiling.

'For a conspiracy theory that seems to be going nowhere, suddenly we're inundated by spooks.'

After Callum had stopped laughing he suggested they take their leave of the pub and have a walk by the sea.

'It's freezing out there Callum!'

'These walls have ears my son,' replied Callum, stepping off the bar-stool.

Collar's up against the biting wind the two men walked eastward towards Newhaven Harbour.

'So, what is so important that you couldn't tell me in the comfort of the pub?' asked Tod.

'Do you know what all this means?'

'I haven't a clue,' answered Tod.

'There are low clouds on the horizon and they are forming at the leading edge of a thunderstorm.'

'Cut with the William Blake metaphors Callum. What does it all mean?'

'Thanks to Bayani, we are now involved in something that is much bigger than you and me and much bigger than JP Associates and Police Scotland. There is nothing allegorical about storm clouds, especially clouds that derive from a sea breeze. I thought you of all people would see the comparison. Maybe you should take a closer look at the new acquisition in your office. I'm sure Valerie would enlighten you on the links between metaphor and reality in her work.'

'Callum, we're talking about a finance company, one whose driving force is mere profit. What has this got to do with storm clouds, an eighteenth-century poet, and a twenty-first century painter?'

'Yes, and that company has named itself after those clouds and I am talking about the work of the twenty-first century painter, namely your Valerie. Have you checked out the cloud formation in the work she presented to you?'

'Listen Callum, why don't you just spit it out. Are we on to something here or are we just pissing in the wind? Whatever you are on about, Valerie cannot possibly be involved. We only met recently, and she is a community artist working for the Scottish Government.' Tod's outburst was more imperative than mere comment. 'I'm getting tired of the intrigue Callum, in fact I'm calling it a night.'

'You know what they did with Wordsworth to silence him, don't you? They gave him a job with the government.'

Before Tod could respond Callum had crossed the road and was striding out towards the pub. Callum smiled to himself, knowing full well it was the mention of Valerie, in relation to their conspiracy, which had made Tod so uncomfortable and brought on his sudden wave of panic. Now he knew Tod would not let this go, until it had reached its full conclusion.

CHAPTER ELEVEN

Tuesday 18th November

Tod phoned Valerie early the next morning and offered to buy her breakfast by the harbour. She declined his offer as she was busy packing to catch the Lewis Ferry from Ullapool that afternoon. But Tod quickly pointed out that a good breakfast would mean she wouldn't have to stop for lunch and the breakfast was on him.

'I wanted to talk to you about the painting you gave us,' said Tod, once they'd collected their buffet breakfast from the counter.

'And I was thinking it was my stimulating company you were after,' she responded. 'This breakfast looks good.'

'I do want to see you but also want to learn a wee bit more about the picture hanging in our office.'

'Why? What are you up to now Dougal?' Valerie leaned forward and felt under his hairline. 'I can just about feel those horns.' Every time she made this reference to Muriel Spark's devil-like character Dougal Douglas it made Tod laugh.

'Okay, you've got me sussed. A friend of mine was talking about the painting, which I assume he's seen hanging in the office. He was making reference to the storm clouds in your work. He raised the subject of allegory, particularly with reference to William Blake and I wanted to know from the horse's mouth if that was an intentional device by the artist herself.'

'Horse's mouth! I've been called many a thing in the past but a horse, no that's a first!'

'Sorry, I didn't mean...'

'For one moment I was beginning to think you'd spotted the deliberate mistake.'

'Pardon?' questioned Tod.

'Just joking. I hate to disappoint you Douglas, but I'm afraid there is no attempt at allegory in that painting, religious or otherwise. It's just about truth as seen through the eyes of a lowly Leith painter. The clouds are there most of the time when I look out from my window, as are the oil-rigs and the pleasure craft and fishing boats.'

'I met a fisherman the other night in the Starbank. He has a lobster boat in the harbour.'

'That might be the same man I see going out in all weathers to lay his creels. He looks a fair age actually.'

'That could be him. Callum said he is one of the best sailors he's ever met.'

'Callum?' she asked.

'Callum Mackie.'

'Would that be the Reverend Callum Mackie, by any chance?'

'The very one. Do you know him?'

'Oh aye, I know him alright and I'll wager he's the friend who suggested you may find allegory in my painting.'

'That's right, but how do you know him?'

'Callum was involved in the celebrations we had when we left Fort House. He was very interested in my work; in fact, he bought a small watercolour of the harbour from me.'

'So he does have an interest in your work?'

'More of an interest in me actually, if my instinct is still intact and I don't sound too conceited. He probably knows you and I are an item and was just letting you know he knows me too.'

'An item? Never thought I'd find myself on a shopping list. Are we an item?'

'How many men do you think I allow into my flat to view my etchings? He is a bit of a looker mind that Callum, for his age anyway.'

'Don't tell me you prefer older men?'

'You tell me, old man,' said Valerie, standing up to refill her coffee.

After breakfast Tod went straight to the office. It was still only ten-thirty and he had two hours to await the onslaught that was sure to come. He knew Tracey had not been overjoyed at Harry's incarceration in police custody but hoped he could calm the situation when he pointed out that her husband had been released, without charge. The best move before that moment came, he thought, was to pay a visit to Jake at his bench. He was in no doubt that Jake would be there, despite the fact that a freezing cold north wind was blowing its way up Constitution Street and turning many faces to fists.

When he got to the bench he could see Jake had already received his coffee delivery from Mark. However, there was no sign of the young man and Tod assumed, rightly as it turned out, that he was back waiting table in the cafe.

'That looks nice', said Tod as he sat down.

'Dae ye want me tae go and get ye one?' asked Jake.

'No, you're alright, I've had breakfast.'

'Brewers Fayre?'

'Aw Jake, how can you possibly know that?'

'Ma laddie was picking somebody up in his taxi at the Premier Inn and thought he saw ye leaving wie that eh...what's her name.'

'Valerie,' said Tod. 'You know Jake, sometimes I get the feeling that everyone around here knows more about my life than I do. I'm getting information from all and sundry and can't quite figure out who knows what and how they are getting their information.'

'That's terrible son,' said Jake. 'Was it not like that in North Telford when ye worked there? Dae you no wish ye were back there now, strutting your stuff as a community worker and saving the deprived? That's what they call them eh, the deprived.'

Tod didn't take the bait with the reference to his old job. 'Have you managed to find anything out about the case we discussed in the office?' asked Tod.

'What case?'

'You know what I mean, the discussion about the oil-rig supply ships.'

'Oh that, aye! A've done some asking around; A've even talked wie a skipper of a tug that bring the monsters in tae port, but he thinks your theory is aw mince. He says the work these boats dae is worth mair than any drugs or precious stanes or anything else ye could bring in illegally and he's been around long enough tae ken.'

'I'm beginning to wonder if this whole thing is nothing more than some fantasy dreamed up by the sailor I spoke with that night at the party.'.

'Maybe he was on drugs? It's looking like that right enough. Are ye just going tae call it a day then?'

'I think so Jake. In fact, why don't we just call it a day here and now?'

'Good idea. Are ye going tae call another meeting tae tell everybody else?'

'Do you think that is necessary?'

'Well we wouldnae want wee Harry going and daen something reckless when we've dropped the case.'

'How do you know about...? No, don't answer that,' said Tod, standing to take his leave.

Once Tod was away Mark reappeared and took a seat beside Jake.

'What was your idea Jake?'

'It's a tried and tested method that A've used in the past. It's a methodology that was used in our last case and it lead to the receiving of information that helped solve that case.'

'Methodology? Have you been on one of Tod's Community Education courses? That case was never really solved, was it Jake,' said Mark. 'and they never did find out exactly what happened to Karl either.'

'You've got a point there son. I am sorry about Karl.' Jake paused for a moment. 'Anywie, the idea is that you and I go down to Ocean Terminal any weekday around lunchtime and stand wie our collecting tins until we see the office workers coming fae the direction of the port authority offices. We focus our attention on them and while we're helping them tae part wie their hard-earned cash, we interview them about working for the port authority. It's surprising what information ye can gather that way.'

'Now that is an interesting idea. I could even use that method of research for my psychology PhD. What agency will we be collecting for?'

'The last time we used this method we decided on a literacy charity, but that might not work wie the office wallahs. A was thinking something mair tae dae wie a charity for redundant surveyors.'

'You're not serious?'

'No, A was only joking. A thought we'd just use the same gear as last time.'

'Sounds great but my first day off isn't until next Monday,' said Mark, keen to get on with the job. His enthusiasm nearly caused him to forget one important item, but not quite. 'Will JP Associates pay me for this one?'

'No Son, not for the moment anywie. But dinnae you go worrying about that, A'll make sure ye get your expenses. How much dae they pay you?'

'Twenty-five pounds an hour.'

'Aw right. Well it should only take us about half an hour, if you're as good as they say you are? So that should be about twelve quid.'

'I've got to get there and recap afterwards Jake, that will take at least another two hours. By the way, why are we keeping it a secret from Tod?'

'Och, ye ken what he's like, he'd just go worrying himself.'

As Tod sat in the office worrying himself about what Jake might be up to, and Tracey's coming onslaught, Bob was getting his share of grief from his DI in Fettes Command Centre.

'Did you know that Harry Cowan, the husband of your secretary Tracey, was arrested at the weekend?'

'Who?'

'Don't give me that Bob James. I remember you took a phone call the last time we spoke, that would be about the same time Harry Cowan was sitting in a Constitution Street cell. After that phone call you immediately cut our meeting short, without a by your leave, and rushed off into the wide blue yonder. I have no doubt you went in the direction of Leith. So, are you going to tell me what's going on or do I have to get the thumb screws out?'

'What is this Sandra, the third degree? That phone-call was nothing and the reason I rushed away was I thought I'd left the cooker on at home.'

'Early signs of dementia eh. What was the phone-call about?'

'It was probably a wrong number.'

'Have you got your phone with you?' she asked.

'My phone, you'll not believe it, but it must have fallen out of my jacket. I haven't seen it since that day.' He reached into his jacket pocket and produced a mobile phone. 'I picked up this wee pay-as-you-go. I'll need to give you the number.'

'You think you've got all the answers Bobby, but I can tell you, you haven't! What happened to the phone we gave you when you took this job?'

Sandra's use of the familiar "Bobby" was a subtle reference to his relationship with Rebecca as she was the only one who called him that. But Sandra's didn't know Bob as well as she thought and her attempt at ridicule may just have let him off the hook.

'Well if you must know, it was Rebecca who called. You know we've not seen much of each other recently and she wanted to see me. I just didn't want to share that information, not even with you.'

'So darling Rebecca calls and the big man just drops everything and goes running, is that it?' said Sandra.

'Something like that.'

'Well I don't believe it. Was it Tod who called?'

'Tod? No, I've warned him not to involve me in JP Associates when I'm working on a cold case, what with the possibility of a conflict of interest and all that.'

As Bob said this he immediately regretted it. He liked and respected DI Sandra Laing and knew from the look on her face he'd stepped over the mark. Sandra Laing was one of the most experienced officers on the force and had come up against enough intrigue to be able to smell a rat a mile off. And if someone held out on her, she was famed for returning the compliment. She began walking away from his desk then suddenly turned round.

'Has your friend managed to kick his nasty habit yet Bob?'

'What's all this about now Sandra?'

'I was just wondering.'

'As far as I know he has come off the drugs. Sandra are you trying to tell me something?'

'It was just something that came up the day we interviewed him for receiving drugs.'

'What was that?'

'Oh, it's not important, I was just wondering.'

The onslaught that Tod had been expecting from Tracey didn't materialise, and neither did she. She phoned at noon to say that she wasn't feeling very well and would be taking the rest of the week off. Tracey had never lost one day at work since she's started with JP Associates at the beginning of the year and when Tod had asked her what the problem was she would only say she didn't feel too well. This reply came at Tod much worse than the rebuke for involving Harry in criminal activities. He resisted the urge to ask any more questions, particularly over the phone. When she hung up he was left assuming it was Harry's arrest that had caused her sudden ill-health. He couldn't be further from the truth.

After leaving Bob and Tod in the Shore Bar on the Monday afternoon, Harry had made his way to the Anchor Inn in Granton. The Anchor was one of his old haunts and he could always guarantee a listening ear for his recent exploits. After six pints of lager and four recitals of his tale, he'd decided to make his way home. Unfortunately, he didn't make it and didn't see Tracey until she came to pick him up from Accident and Emergency at the Western General Hospital early the next day.

When she got there at three in the morning Harry was sitting in the waiting room adjacent to reception. He was badly bruised and the numerous cuts on his face had required stitches. She could see he'd been crying.

'What happened Harry?'

'A'm sorry Trace.'

'Oh, you're sorry. No half as sorry as the people who did this to you will be, A can tell ye that.'

Harry tried a smile. 'Now, we'll not have any of that. Remember, you've learned tae turn the other cheek.'

'No, not this time Harry. Naebody daes that tae ma man and gets away with it.' She touched his cheek.

'You'd better wait till ye hear the whole story.'

'And then she asked me if you were managing to come off the drugs,' said Bob, as he waited for their order at the bar.

'How strange,' replied Tod.

'Not as strange as her asking if you had children, and in particular, daughters.'

The second Bob said that, Tod knew exactly what his DI had been referring to. It was over a year ago now but during his interview, about receiving class A drugs, the DI had become very interested in the fact that he'd bought the same kind and same amount of drug that had killed Richard Stark. By asking Bob if Tod had any daughters, she was still trying to place him closer to Stark's murder. DI Laing was looking for motive and if Tod had had a daughter it may have been possible that Stark had molested her. That would be motive enough.

'She's a bit of a weird one, that DI of yours. Is she thinking if I'd had a family I wouldn't have got involved in drugs?'

'She said it was something that had come up during your interview.'

'Mm. She did seem concerned about my immediate future, you know my job and so on. Maybe she is still wondering how my situation has affected me.'

'Aye, maybe she is. She does have a motherly streak,

115

when it suits her. On the other hand, why would she ask if you had daughters? Sons would be as badly affected by your situation.' Bob thought for a moment. 'Either way, it will come out in the wash if I know our Sandra, that's for sure.'

Harry explained that he'd been on his way home from the Anchor Inn around nine when three men pushed him down the stairs by the supermarket and followed him down. They hadn't given any reason for their actions, leaving him to believe it must have been a case of mistaken identity. He still didn't explain to Tracey what he'd been up to in the early hours of Sunday morning or about his sojourn in Constitution Street nick.

'This is maybe not the time Harry, but why did ye decide tae leave the house in the early hours of Sunday morning and break intae that office?'

'A couldnae sleep darling, so A had a walk intae Leith. Ye ken what A'm like. A got tae thinking about Tod and his need for information so decided tae get him some. It was nothing tae dae wie him, honest darling.'

'Oh, A ken what ye're like Harry Cowan. You'll never change. It was a gie long walk mind, ye didnae come back till now.'

'Oh aye,' replied Harry. 'Sorry darling.'

CHAPTER TWELVE

Thursday 20th November

Tracey still hadn't appeared for work by the Thursday, by which time Tod was climbing the walls. Bob's revelation that his DI was asking questions relating to Tod's drug arrest and that she'd asked whether Tod had any daughters, worried him too. Those questions could be related to the murder of Richard Stark. The fact that Bob remained unaware of this was neither here nor there; it was really only a matter of time before he cottoned on.

By twelve-fifty Tod couldn't bear it any longer and was just about to pick up the phone and call Tracey, when the office door opened.

'Tracey, how are you?' he asked, putting down the phone and crossing the office to greet her. 'I was just about to phone you.'

For one moment she thought Tod was going to give her a hug. 'A'm alright,' she said, dodging past him.

'Tracey, I...'

'I don't want to know Tod, if ye dinnae mind. Ma Harry is laid up in bed and he is no well. And it's all because of you!'

'Tracey, please believe me, I didn't ask Harry to do anything illegal for JP Associates.'

117

'Maybe not, but it was enough for Harry tae think ye needed it done. He's loyal tae you Tod and he wanted tae help. You've got a great way to get people tae dae your bidding, without striking a blow yourself. You were always the same, even when you were teaching parents at their bairns' schools, they'd dae anything for ye, and always for nothing!'

'Just a minute Tracey...' Tod stopped in his tracks...'why is Harry laid up in bed? Did he catch what you had?'

'No, I thought you'd know. Harry got beaten up on Monday night outside the Anchor. He's in an awfie mess.'

'I haven't heard. I am so sorry Tracey. Are the police involved?'

'No, the polis are not involved. He disnae want them involved in case they decide tae charge you wie the break-in.'

'I'll phone Bob,' said Tod.

'You'll no bother, A've already made arrangements tae have it sorted.'

'Have you contacted your preacher?'

'No, A've made an appointment wie the jail tae see Jimmy McGuire on Saturday.'

'What! Tracey, you can't do that. Revenge is never as sweet as one imagines.' As Tod said this, his mind travelled back across his own moments of revenge. 'What about your faith?'

'Dinnae you get all sanctimonious on me. Naebody, and A mean naebody does that tae ma Harry and gets away with it.'

Tracey would have been as well talking to the wall. Tod was an expert on revenge and its consequences. 'Harry will heal Tracey and it will soon be forgotten, with no ill consequences.'

'A don't think you understand boss. They had a gun and they threatened tae shoot him. Harry was really scared; mair frightened than he's ever been.'

CHAPTER THIRTEEN

Saturday 22nd November

Jimmy McGuire and Tracey sat opposite each other at their usual table in the Visitors' Area of Edinburgh Prison. A book lay between them on the table.

'How are getting on wie the reading Jimmy?' she asked him.

Jimmy looked around to see that no-one could hear the subject of their conversation. His dyslexia was not a subject for sharing, even though more than half the prison population shared the same condition. 'Great hen,' he whispered. 'Your letters have been brilliant and the Glasgow Bible ye left me has me reading like a man possessed.' He laid his hand on the book and looked directly at her. 'Having something written down in your ain language really does help. The Broons and Oor Wullie were about the only two things A read when A was wee. How have you been getting on? It's been a wee while since A've seen ye.'

'Aw right,' answered Tracey.

'Aw right? A dinnae think so hen. What is bothering you?'

'It's not so much what but mair "who". It's got me in turmoil.'

'What's happened?'

'Ma man Harry got arrested for burglary in the early hours of Monday morning but was released in the afternoon, without charge. Then he went for a pint tae the Anchor Inn...'

The old man smiled before interrupting her. 'A've no been in the Anchor for years.'

'Aye well, when he left there he was jumped by three men and beaten up. One had a gun and threatened tae shoot him.' Tears began running down her face.

The sight of her tears caused Jimmy to lean forward and touch her cheek. 'Is he aw right now?'

'Aye, but his confidence is zilch. He'll not go out of the house.'

'What place did Harry break intae?'

'It was the offices of the port authorities in Leith Docks.'

'What did he dae that for? Dae they keep money in the safe?'

'No, it was just something stupid, something for the folk A work with.'

'Oh aye, JP Associates, A remember you work for them. Listen hen, dae ye think the port authorities might be capable of daen that tae Harry?'

'A just dinnae ken what tae think Jimmy. All A ken is Harry isnae the man he was.'

'Dinnae you go worrying yourself too much about Harry; that man of yours is made of stronger stuff than ye think. Fae what A remember of Harry Cowan, he'll soon get his confidence back. So, is it aboot Harry that ye came tae see me?'

'Aye.'

'Ye want me tae dae something about it?'

Tracey hesitated, 'Aye, maybe, A dinnae ken.'

'What about our Lord, dae ye no think He might have something tae say about it?'

'Aye, but tae be honest Jimmy A don't care anymore. A just want the bastards tae pay for what they did to Harry.'

The last of the visiting-hour minutes were taken up with Jimmy trying to convince Tracey that her path and instruction came from the Lord, and that revenge belonged to Him and Him only.

Eventually she agreed and took Jimmy's advice to go straight to her church and pray for guidance. It was only then that she remembered to mention Shifty Stewart and how his name had come up in conversation in JP Associates' office.

'Who's interested?' asked Jimmy.

'No-one in particular, it's just the Reverend Callum Mackie was explaining some stuff to us and said that Mr Stewart had been in here. I just wondered if you'd met him, that's all.'

'Once or twice,' said Jimmy, 'And A've met the good Reverend on many occasions too. Is he working with your associates now?'

'Was he the one who saved you?'

'Aye.' Jimmy was deep in thought before he spoke. 'Stewart was moved fae here tae another jail, somewhere in England A think. That's about aw A can tell ye so ye can tell your bosses that they'll have to get their information elsewhere.'

Tracey smiled but did not reply. When she left Jimmy called the warden over. 'Bill, could you tell Big Grant Thomson tae come tae ma cell, A need tae speak tae him.'

'Certainly Jimmy.'

CHAPTER FOURTEEN

Monday 24th November

Bob was in the Cold Case office by seven on the Monday morning. He wanted to begin his research into the Stewart case in earnest, without interruption. As it was, most of his research would have to be carried out on social media as the police sites all had RESTRICED ACCESS written across them, where Shifty Stewart was concerned anyway.

He found from the numerous newspaper reports that one former inmate who'd served time with Stewart had told the newspapers: "Everyone was surprised that he hadn't gone very far and had died in a squat in London. It seemed remarkable that a rich man would live like that, when he could have been living it up in the sun."

What Bob did glean from the public search-engines was that throughout his adult life, Stewart was never far from controversy. During the sixties he'd worked as a property developer, but it wasn't until the nineteen-eighties that he took his first steps into the world of organised crime. He set himself up as a fence, opening up a jewellery store in Edinburgh, which was used for the disposing of hundreds of thousands of pounds worth of stolen goods.

Within a few years he had begun importing drugs into Scotland using a fleet of boats. One of his many boats, HMV Telemachus, an offshore supply vessel, had previously been used by another drugs gang. Its multimillion-pound illegal cargo was confiscated, and its captain and nine-man crew arrested by customs off the Scottish coast. Bob found this information very interesting indeed and thought to run it by Sandra.

By the time of his trial Stewart was known to own dozens of properties, both here and abroad. He also had stakes in Edinburgh businesses, yet he was granted legal aid to fund his defence. The court found that most of his assets had been transferred into his wife's name and Stewart was only fined one hundred thousand pounds.

When Sandra appeared just after eight, Bob could hardly wait to give her the gist of his findings.

'Are you not going to let me get my coat off Mr James?'

'I wanted to let you know my findings on the Stewart case.'

'Oh that. You shouldn't have bothered. Yes, you've guessed it, there has been a change of plan regarding that case and "it's been shelved", yet again.'

'What! No bloody wonder they call it the Cauld Case Squad, it's that bloody cauld, it's deid. How many cases have we been called off now? Should have called it the Called-off Squad.'

'I know, I know, and I do agree with you this time. In fact, I've put in for a transfer back to the drug squad,' said Sandra.

'You've what? Are you going to let those shites hold back your prospects? Don't let it happen Sandra. Don't think by towing the party line or going back to your old job you'll be doing yourself any favours; you're talking to a man who knows exactly where crawling gets you: bloody nowhere!'

'I hate to contradict you Bob but as far as I remember, you have never crawled in your life, unless of course in your social life?'

'Very funny! What are we going to do about this? Stewart was a bad bugger and there are others, even bigger buggers, who want to remain hidden. We can't collude in that Sandra.'

Sandra walked across to her desk.

'So, what are you going to do about it?' Bob called over.

'Well firstly, I'll ask our consultant what he thinks. Have you any suggestions Mr James?'

'I may have.'

'I thought that might be the case.'

'Let me have a free hand.'

'You mean let JP Associates have a free hand?'

'Aye.'

'What about that conflict of interest you were warned about?'

'Change the tune please boss, it's wearing thin. And talking about tunes, what was that one you were playing the other day when you asked if Tod had any daughters?'

'I told you, it was just something that came up during his interview. I was thinking that if he had a family they'd suffer big-time from the revelations that their Dad was on drugs.'

'But why only daughters?'

'I thought you'd understand that. The bond between daughters and fathers is a close one and a daughter would have been much more likely to suffer from the discovery that her Dad was a drug-addict.'

Bob was not convinced by Sandra's family-psychology lesson but decided to let it stand, for the moment. 'Do I have your permission then?'

Sandra removed her coat and placed it on the back of her chair. 'Yes, but I'll deny that if it comes out.'

'You've nothing to worry about on that score, JP Associates are very discrete.'

'Aye right,' said Sandra. 'Just tread carefully. Now can I get on with some work?'

'Well how did you get on on Saturday?' asked Tod.

'Okay,' answered Tracey.

'Did you go ahead with it?'

'With what?'

'You know what I mean.'

'No I didn't. Jimmy talked me out of it, if you must know.'

'I bet that's a first for Jimmy McGuire. What did he say?'

'I think you know that don't you, boss, if you are honest? He believes in a higher power. Oh, by the way Harry did tell me you had nothing to do with his visit to the port offices.' Tracey made it sound as if Harry had merely been on an excursion, and not on a burglary, but Tod didn't point this out as it looked as if he was about to be let off the hook.

'Did you get a chance to mention Shifty Stewart?'

'Aye, but Jimmy had only met him a couple of times.'

'Oh, I see. That's that then, knowing how much we

can now trust Jimmy McGuire since he found his higher power.'

'Now don't go there. I'm sick of telling you, the man has been reborn!'

'Let me get this straight. He only met Stewart a couple of times. That is very interesting when one bears in mind the fact that Callum swears the two serious criminals were bosom buddies?'

'A'm getting about sick of everyone believing that Jimmy McGuire is a liar Tod. I'm sick telling you, Jimmy McGuire has turned over a new leaf, and that's final!'

As Tracey was storming off to fill the kettle, Big Grant Thomson's henchmen were approaching the port offices. They'd been instructed to ask questions relating to the break-in on the previous Monday and not, under any circumstances, to use threatening behaviour. Their guise, that they were security personnel in the business of helping keep people safe wasn't too far from the truth, depending which way one looked at it. Dougie pressed the intercom.

'Yes?'

'Property Protection PLC' answered the henchman.

'Do you have an appointment?'

'We were instructed by Leith Police to pay you a visit regarding your recent break-in.'

'Oh, of course. I'll just buzz you in and see you at reception.'

When the young man opened one half of the double door he had to look upwards to see Dougie's face, but not for long as the worn and scarred face moved closer to his.

'We need to have a look around son, but before we dae...do that, we need to have a word with your manager.'

'I'm sorry, the office manager is not here, but I could let you have a look around. Will you be checking for flaws in our security system?'

'Aye,' piped up Dougie's comrade at arms, 'the kind of flaws that led tae one of our mates taking a hiding fae you!'

Until that moment Dougie had been priding himself on his behaviour and new found Standard English, but Freddie had just blown that, right out the water. He threw his colleague a look. 'Aw Freddie!' He turned back to the office junior. 'What my colleague here is trying tae say is that somebody in your office took it upon themselves tae see that the bloke who broke intae your place widnae dae it again. Now that means that some of our friends are not happy.' He picked the boy up by the shirt collar. 'Just tell your boss, or whoever might be responsible, that if it happens again we cannie be responsible for our actions! Have ye got that son?'

'Yes, I've got that. I'll tell him when he gets in.'

The office manager was not at his desk during the visit from Grant Thomson's friends, because he'd been held up; he was at that moment trying to avoid the two men who'd accosted him outside Ocean Terminal. They were busy trying to relieve him of his loose change for their collecting tins.

Nick Clark had been with the port authority since its humble beginnings back in nineteen-seventy-seven and looked as if he was on his final furlong. 'I told you, I've already told you, I've only half an hour for lunch and I need to get up that escalator to M&S for my sandwich and back to the office.'

'Half an hour isn't very long for a lunch-break,' added Mark. 'I wouldn't fancy working for your employer.'

'No, you wouldn't; for one thing you never know who "they" are, apart from the occasional visit from some big-shot from somewhere in Europe. I'm left to run the whole shebang. I've been there since I left school. I think I was only given the office manager job to keep my face straight and to stop me complaining about the salary.'

'Who do you work for?' asked Jake.

'The port authorities, for my sins.'

Jake winked at Mark. 'I've heard they are a good employer. Someone I know piloted a tug out of the docks and got a good handshake when he retired.'

'Aye, but your friend would have been out in the Forth Estuary most of the time, not stuck in the office pushing paper and trying to get the staff to do something other than discuss their next night-out.'

'Weren't you guys burgled recently?' asked Jake.

'How do you know that? It stayed out of the news.'

Jake tapped his nose. 'News travels fast in Leith.'

'They caught the perpetrator, but he got off lightly. I'm not sure why.'

'I love the sea,' said Mark. 'Do you have anything to do with those off-shore ships over there?' He pointed over to the huge ships towering over the docks.

'We're responsible for everything and anything that comes within range,' the man replied, proudly.

Jake saw his chance. 'That must be some job and some responsibility. Pleased to meet you.' He put his hand forward. 'I'm Frank and this is my assistant Nigel. As we said, we're collecting on behalf of a literacy charity.'

'Well you ought to get yourselves over to my office; the bairns they're sending me from school now can hardly string two words together, on paper or otherwise.'

'You'll appreciate the importance of our work then,' said Mark, putting forward his tin.

The man took out his wallet. 'The names Nick, Nick Clark.' He put five pounds in Mark's tin. Jake's compliment had got to him. 'Would you be interested in seeing those ships at close-quarters son? You come to the office then take a tour, if you'd like?'

'I would like that very much,' replied Mark enthusiastically.

'What about a week today? It would have to be after work; we're not supposed to be accessible to public scrutiny. Do you know where we are situated?'

'No, but I'm sure I'll find it. Isn't it the building near that old lighthouse supply ship?'

'Yes, that's the one. I'll get it in the office diary. Listen, I'm sorry but I do have to dash.' At that, Nick was off like a bolt out of the blue.

'I think he likes you,' commented Jake.

'Jealous?' asked Mark, smiling.

Alan Addison

CHAPTER FIFTEEN

Tuesday 25th November

Bob had phoned Tod the minute he was given the go-ahead to involve JP Associates in the goings-on around the life and death of Shifty Stewart. They arranged to meet for coffee the next morning.

'Well, what did she actually say?' asked Tod.

'It wasn't so much what she said, more what she didn't say,' answered Bob.

'Oh, I see. It's the official, unofficial go-ahead.'

'Something like that. Nevertheless, it does give us an opportunity to test your theories about sea-monsters, while investigating the death of Shifty Stewart.'

'Test my theories. What's that supposed to mean?'

'Well I think you know what it means,' answered Bob, smiling.

'Okay Inspector let me get this right. You are coming to us for help, is that not the case? So, maybe it's as well for you to keep your ideas to yourself regarding what you think of our theories, and methods come to that, wouldn't you agree?'

'Don't take life so seriously me auld mucker, I was only pulling your leg. We might have to ask Tracey if she wouldn't mind raising the subject of Stewart with Jimmy McGuire. What do you think?'

'So, you're not too worried about her visiting him in prison now that it suits your Cold Case?'

'Well she is visiting him regardless, isn't she?'

'Actually, she visited him on Saturday. I was a bit concerned to be honest, particularly after Harry was beaten up. I thought she was going to ask McGuire to intervene on her behalf.'

'And did she?'

'I don't think so. Well the truth is, she said McGuire talked her out of revenge.'

'For goodness sake Tod, what have you got us involved in now? "Jimmy McGuire talked her out of revenge". No, that's not how it would have played out. His, or someone else's henchmen will be seeing to her request, probably as we speak. Sometimes I can't believe just how naïve you are. How many times have I told you that Jimmy McGuire is a bloody gangster. I can hardly believe this. What a nightmare!'

CHAPTER SIXTEEN

Friday 28th November

The first Jake knew of what happened to Nick Clark, Office Manager to the port authorities, was when Mark appeared at Jake's bench. He was as white as a ghost.

'You look like you've seen a ghost Mark,' said Jake.

'I think we might. Have you listened to the news this morning?'

'No, I get all my news sitting here.' Jake patted his bench lovingly.

'Well maybe not all of it. The man we met the other day at Ocean Terminal, Nick Clark, he's been found dead and in a terrible mess. His body was cut all over and displayed across the old whaling harpoon gun on the Shore, like some sort of trophy.' Mark was shaking.

'Columbian drug cartels have been known to display their victims as works of art. I think they call it Columbian Art maybe,' said Jake.

'Do you not think it's an awful coincidence that we were only speaking to him on Monday and the subject of the oil supply ships came up and now the man has been murdered? Do you think it could be to do with some environmental group which objects against the use of fossil fuels, in this case oil?'

'A think it's more probably tae dae wie a group that burgled the port offices last week.'

'What's that all about?'

'You don't know of course son. Harry was beaten up after a clandestine visit tae the port offices. Tod was just telling me yesterday that Tracey spoke to Jimmy McGuire about getting revenge. He must be reading the Auld Testament in his new-found faith because it looks like he's more than capable of an "eye for an eye".'

'How have we managed to get ourselves so involved?' asked Mark, more a plea than a question. I was due to meet the man next Monday and my name will be in his office diary. What am I going to do?'

'Absolutely nothing! You told him your name was Nigel and that you were interested in the oil industry and Nick was going to give you the grand tour.'

'But we met him when we were collecting for charity under false pretences. The police are bound to find out about that.'

'How are they going to find out about that? The man was on his way tae buy his lunch, that's all.'

'I'm not convinced,' answered Mark.

When the news about the murder came from

Constitution Street Police Station to Fettes, Bob was in the canteen, enjoying his first bacon roll for at least a fortnight. DS John Mackay was the unfortunate who received the news and he delivered it to his former DI. If Brownie points were what he expected, they didn't materialise.

'I thought you'd like to hear the latest from your agency's patch,' he said, sitting down opposite Bob. John was aware, as were the rest of his colleagues, that Bob ran a private investigation agency in Leith.

'Don't tell me, some casuals got bevvied last night and pissed on Queen Victoria's statue,' replied Bob between mouthfuls.

'Not quite. The port office manager, a Nick Clark, was found strapped to the whaling gun on the Shore. He'd been sliced to shreds by a knife of some sort and his body was left there for all to see. He was found early this morning by a cleaner on her way to work. It's been on the radio.' John Mackay could have no idea what he'd just let himself in for by being the bearer of this news.

Bob put down the remains of his bacon roll and looked the young detective in the eye. 'Say that again.'

After John had told the story once more, already getting the drift that he had moved into unchartered waters, Bob swept his arm across the table, scattering his plate, the sauce bottle and his unfinished roll across the canteen floor. He stood up. 'Is this a fucking wind-up?'

'I don't understand,' said John, unsure whether to sit it out or run.

Bob sat down again.

'Are you all right Sir?'

'What have I told you about addressing Mr James as "Sir" DS Mackay!' interrupted DI Sandra Laing, already late for her brunch and not in a very good mood by all accounts. 'John could you give Mr James and me a minute please.' It wasn't a question.

Once John was out of earshot Sandra turned on Bob. 'Have you heard the news?'

'Aye, John just told me.'

'I thought that might be the case from the mess you've made of the floor. Now before I begin, let's dispense with any ideas you may have about Einstein and his theory on coincidences, right!'

'Sandra, I've only found out about this, I don't know what to think.'

'So, the famed Bob James doesn't know what to think. My oh my, that's a new one on me,' stormed Sandra. 'What about you think along the lines that one of your cronies from that Mickey Mouse agency you run in Leith breaks into the port offices. Then he is beaten up. Then his wife pays a visit to Jimmy McGuire in prison. Then, surprise, surprise, the port office manager ends up as a sculpture decorating the waterfront. Now, let me think, I wonder what could be going on here? Or am I missing something Mr James?'

'I know how this must look to you Sandra but let's not jump to too many conclusions. By the way, how did you find out about Harry being beaten up and Tracey visiting McGuire?'

'Do you honestly think I'm buttoned up the back? And, by the way, we can dispense with the "Sandra": it's Detective Inspector Laing to you from now on Mr James and I am not jumping to any conclusions. You are up to your neck in this and so are your cronies and I am going to have them in, one by one, and we'll see exactly what is going on. Maybe that will give you something to think about.' Sandra pointed at the floor. 'And get this bloody mess cleaned up before I get it done and send you the bill!'

As Bob began picking up his breakfast from the floor, the serving lady from behind the counter came up with a dustpan and brush and black plastic bag. 'Didn't think much of my bacon roll Inspector. It's been a while since I've seen you do that. You get yourself away and deal with whatever the volcano has just thrown up. I'll get this tidied.'

'Thanks Mary.' Bob was barely out of the canteen before he phoned Edinburgh Prison to arrange an appointment.

As he was doing that, Sandra was phoning Constitution Street Police Station. Her reputation as someone not to be ignored meant that two constables, one male, one female, were on their way to JP Associates before she had put the phone down.

It was late morning and Tod was the only one in the office. If Tracey had known what was about to happen at that moment she'd have been glad her shift didn't begin until twelve-thirty. The police officers had been instructed to deliver anyone, colleague, associate, or otherwise of Bob James to Fettes Command Centre asap.

Tod had not yet heard about the port office manager's death and had no idea why two police officers had just walked into his office, or why they wanted to take him to Fettes. No doubt Bob James would be waiting for him there.

'Did Bob James send you to get me?' he asked from the rear of the car.

No answer was forthcoming, leading him to believe that his previous crimes had come to light.

As the car pulled into Fettes car-park the young male constables turned. 'Citizen James does not instruct the Leith Police as far as I'm aware.'

This information calmed Tod slightly until the other police officer opened his door. 'You'll no doubt be hoping it was your friend who requested your company sir. Unfortunately for you though it was not. DI Sandra Laing is waiting for you at reception.

Tod was surprised to be met by a smile when he was escorted into the reception area of Fettes Command Centre. DI Laing approached him and put out her hand to shake his. 'It was nice of you to agree to join us Mr Peterson.'

'I don't think "agree" is actually the correct terminology in this instance Inspector, do you?' replied Tod.

'Now, let's not get off on the wrong footing, particularly over mere semantic gestures. Oh, but then I forgot, you're a literature man, aren't you?'

Before he could answer DI Laing put her hand under his elbow and escorted him along the corridor towards the interview rooms.

'We'll see if we can get you the same room as last time, familiarity, and all that.'

'It can breed contempt, Inspector, of one is not

careful,' replied Tod, as he was ushered into the room.

To his surprise DC Margaret Whalen was sitting behind the desk. She too wore a broad smile. 'Well, if it isn't Thomas Peterson,' she said as if surprised to see him. 'This is becoming a regular occurrence, is it not.'

'We can dispense with the formalities Margaret,' said the DI. 'Mr Peterson wouldn't mind if we called him by his nickname. Would that be alright with you, Tod?'

'I learned just last week on my course that "Tod" is the Scottish name for the devil, isn't that right?' asked DC Whalen.

'Is that the best you can do Constable?' commented Tod. 'Bob did say you were studying literature. If you'd like any hints and tips, just say.'

'I believe you have a first from Cambridge.' Margaret tried to sound mocking but Tod could see she was impressed.

Sandra didn't like the way this conversation was going. During Tod's first interview with the two detectives, Margaret had all but been at Tod's throat and now, due to her new-found love of literature, here she was snuggling up to him, albeit verbally. 'I think we can dispense with University Challenge for the moment, don't you Margaret.' She turned to Tod. 'Do you

know why you are here?'

'I have no idea,' answered Tod. 'Is it about my family life?'

'We can cross that bridge when we come to it and I can assure you, we will. There is something linking this morning's event to Brian Hopper's murder.'

'This morning's event? What event?' asked Tod, bewildered.

'Don't tell me the super-fast Leith grapevine hasn't reached the door of JP Associates yet,' intervened Margaret.

'Honestly, I've no idea what you are talking about.'

'The body of Nick Clark, office manager at the port offices, was found draped over the whaling gun by the Shore at five this morning. He had been sliced and mutilated by a knife. Do you remember it was a knife that did for Hopper?'

'What has that got to do with me?' asked Tod, trying to recover from the shock of the news and his mind immediately turning to Tracey's visit to McGuire.'

'He has a wife, children and grandchildren and was about to retire,' said the DI.

A silence fell over the room before she continued. 'You know as well as I do that your secretary's husband was arrested, having broken into the port offices, and was beaten up soon after. You also know that Tracey

Cowan visited Jimmy McGuire in prison on Saturday. And if that is not enough, we've found your associate's name, Nigel, in the port office diary. Apparently, your Nigel was collecting money under false pretences outside Ocean Terminal. He was due to meet with Mr Clark next Monday lunch-time.' The DI leaned back in her chair.

'Have you anything to say?' asked DC Whalen.

'I still don't understand what this has to do with me, nor JP Associates for that matter and I don't know any Nigel.'

'For Nigel read Mark le Mot, your researcher. We've been asking questions Mr Peterson and the staff at Ocean Terminal have been very helpful, as have the CCTV cameras. Tell me, have you ever heard of a William Stewart?' Sandra's quick change of subject caught Tod completely off-guard.

He was about to lie again when he remembered that Bob had been given the unofficial go-ahead by DI Laing to allow JP Associates on the case. 'As a matter of fact, I have heard of him: Bob mentioned him just the other day.'

'What?' asked the DC. 'I have no knowledge of this. Is JP Associates involved in the Stewart case?' She stood up and looked down at her boss.

'Please sit-down Margaret before you get dizzy,' said

the DI, trying to mask her fear of reprimand for instigating a conflict of interest.

'What has William Stewart got to do with the murder of the office manager?' asked Tod.

'Who the bloody hell is doing this interview!' shouted Sandra. 'I'll ask the questions!' She changed tack again abruptly. 'Mr Peterson, as your earlier question acknowledged, you are aware that I have been asking questions about your family and I think you know why. You see, I am convinced that you were involved in the Stark murder. The drugs found on you; the same amount and type of drugs that killed Stark, was not mere coincidence. Bob denies ever telling you about the contents of Starks' house on the night of his murder, yet you had knowledge of those contents when we interviewed you after the event. That information was not public knowledge. As to the question of you having a daughter, if you had a daughter and she had been molested by Stark or his paedophile ring then that may have been enough of a motive for you to want him dead. So, let's be clear on this, I have not removed your name from my enquiries into his death nor the death of Brian Hopper, your supplier. And now another man is found brutally murdered: a man who you have connections with. And he is butchered by a knife, as Hopper was. Now, let me tell you Mr Literature Man, you are sailing very close to the wind and if I were you I'd be very careful what I say.'

Tod assumed wrongly, that he could give as good as he got. 'I thought the official verdict on Richard Stark's death was suicide,' he said in answer.

'I'd forgotten how much of a smart-arse Tod could be, didn't you Margaret. I suppose that must come from being in such a close relationship with ex-Detective Inspector Bob James. You obviously have all the information to hand and all the answers you require too.'

'It would appear that way to me too.' Margaret added, still smarting from the news that JP Associates had been brought on board without her knowledge.

'Why did you assume that this interview was about Stark and Hopper?' asked the DI, turning to Tod.

'Pardon?'

'When you first sat down you wanted to know why I'd been asking about your family. That can only mean you have worked out why.'

'That was because I didn't know about the death of the office manager and thought you'd asked me in to get some background detail about Bob's partner in the business. Am I going to need a lawyer here?'

'Ever the quick thinker Tod. You'll not be needing a lawyer for the moment,' answered the DI, 'but we do require you to make a list of all those working with JP

Associates, whether they are on your books or merely affiliated in some way and we'll need that now!'

Bob had managed to get an appointment to see Jimmy McGuire that afternoon. Although now a mere citizen, old friends in the prison service made sure he had the use of a private interview room.

'They use this room to allow prisoners their conjugal rights,' said Jimmy McGuire when he was escorted in. 'That's no why you're here, is it?'

'Still the same old comedian, eh Jimmy,' replied Bob. 'You always liked a laugh, as I remember; it's a shame it was always at the expense of somebody else.'

'Aye, and still the same auld Bob James, but without the title Inspector.'

'A wee bird tells me you've turned over a new leaf, seen the light and all that.'

'A widnae go calling your secretary a "wee bird". Is that no a bit misogynistic in pc parlance? Anyway, what can this wee comedian dae for ye Mr James?'

'Your vocabulary has certainly come a long way from the Fort days Jimmy. The last time we met you could hardly string two words together.'

'A've a good literacy teacher.'

'Aye, so I've heard,' replied Bob, sitting down.

'I take it you're here to find out what you can about Shifty Stewart. Obviously, your informant didn't manage to get the information you need on her last visit.'

'I'll come to that. I'm here about something else entirely, something even closer to home. When Tracey visited you last Saturday, did she ask you to help her repay the blokes who set about Harry, her man?'

'What blokes? A've nae idea what you're talking about.' The smile Jimmy had worn since entering the room had not yet left his face.

'Jimmy, I know you better than that. I also know that her intention was to speak to you about it.'

'Well, seeing you're not just anybody, the lassie did mention that Harry had been done-up, but she never mentioned reprisals. Like me she is a Christian and believes that vengeance belongs tae our Lord.'

'Right, let's cut the crap for a minute McGuire. Are you responsible for the visit those two thugs made to the port offices last week? Do you know they threatened a young lad in the office?'

'You're definitely barking up the wrong tree Mr James. A've nae idea what you're talking about. As you can see from our surroundings, A'm banged-up. Even if A had wanted tae get involved A'd have a hard job, don't ye think?' Jimmy paused for a few seconds. 'What A dinnae understand though is why ye would bother coming tae see me cause a wee laddie was threatened in the port offices. Should you no be taking your retirement a wee bit mair seriously than that and getting yourself a wee security job. A could recommend ye.'

'Those heavies that you organised to visit the port offices have done something much worse than insult a wee laddie. It would appear their enthusiasm holds no bounds.' Bob stood up again.

'Humour me Inspector, just for auld-times sake. What have my imaginary friends supposed tae have done?'

'Oh, nothing drastic Jimmy; they've only gone and sliced up the manager of the port offices and left him deid.'

The smile left Jimmy McGuires face for the first time. Bob thought to question him more but had a change of heart, walked to the door and knocked. As he left, a prison officer entered the room. Bob could hear the prisoner shout at the top of his voice. 'Get Grant Thompson along here Walter and dinnae take no for an answer!'

It was Bob's turn to smile as he walked through the hall.

CHAPTER SEVENTEEN

Monday 1st December

'I'd just wrapped the grandbairn's advent calendar and was getting ready for church yesterday morning, when there was a loud knock on my front door. A nearly jumped out my skin. The last people A expected to see when I opened the door were two polismen. A thought they must have been here tae see Harry and query him about the burglary, or the mugging. What can A dae for you officers I asked. "You can get your coat love and come with us to Fettes", said the taller of the two. Harry's not been out for over a week, A said. "It's not Harry we're here for, it's you". Then he had second thoughts for a minute and asked, "Are you Tracey Cowan, secretary to JP Associates in Great Junction Street, Leith"? I am that, A answered. "Right, get your coat", he said. But I was just about to go to the church, A said, but he wisnae listening.'

'I am so sorry I got you involved in this whole affair Tracey,' said Tod. 'If I had just kept my mouth shut about Bayani and his deep-sea fantasies, none of this would have happened.'

'Och, don't worry yourself about that. A'm glad you got us involved and I'm going to see this through.'

'That's a change of heart, is it not. It was only the other day you were accusing me of leading you all astray.'

'That was before Detective Inspector Laing tried to reduce me to the position of wee girly. She, and her pal DC Whalen spoke to me like I was glaikit, and A'm no having that. They wouldnae even tell me what they were questioning me about. She wanted tae know aw about ma visits tae Jimmy McGuire. A think she was just trying tae find out more about JP Associates, particularly you. Maybe it's that "conflict of interest" that Bob's always banging on about. Either way, we are going to see this project through to the end, whether we find a grand hooded phantom or not.'

'Bob's been to see Jimmy McGuire.' Tod turned to look for distraction as he said this, and rightly so.

'What?' Tracey took hold of his arm.

'Bob, he's been to see McGuire.' Tod could see Tracey's defences rising.

'What about? Is it anything to do with me?'

'Tracey, tell me honestly, did you ask for Jimmy McGuire's help in finding the men who beat up Harry?'

'Oh, I see. If you must know, I only mentioned it on the passing, but Jimmy talked me out of it. A didnae really want anybody tae get hurt, even though ma Harry is still feared tae leave the house. What's aw the fuss about anyway?'

Tod wasn't sure how Tracey would take the news

that the office manager had been brutally murdered.

'Tod Peterson, are you gonnae tell me what's going on, or are you gonnae treat me like Inspector Laing did yesterday? A need tae know what's happening!'

Tod turned to face her. 'Nick Clark, the manager of the offices that Harry burgled was found murdered early on Friday morning. He had been butchered and left like a piece of meat across the whaling gun on the Shore.'

Tracey slumped down at the coffee table but didn't speak.

'Are you all right?' Tod sat down opposite her.

'A don't understand, what's his murder that got tae dae wie me?'

'If you told Jimmy McGuire about Harry being mugged just after he'd broken in to their offices, then it has quite a lot to do with you Tracey. It's possible McGuire organised the murder.'

She didn't reply but sat quietly, staring at the wall opposite, before slowly rising from her chair and walking to the coat stand.

'Tracey, I told you nothing good would come from you befriending McGuire.'

She began crying as she struggled to put on her coat.

Tod tried to put his hand on her arm but she shrugged him off and, with coat only half on and without another word, rushed out of the office.

Tod immediately phoned Bob, but there was no reply. After leaving a message telling him about Tracey's reaction to the news, he decided to phone Callum.

'Aye, I'm in the Quiet Room at Ocean Terminal, do you want to join me here?'

'I'll be with you within half an hour,' replied Tod.

When he got to the door of the quiet room a woman was just leaving. She'd obviously been crying and was holding a hanky to her face. Tod was about to speak but thought better of it. When he walked in, Callum was leaning on the window sill, staring out at the Royal Yacht Britannia and across the quay to the Flour Mill.

'That woman looked upset,' commented Tod.

Callum didn't turn around. 'That was Nick Clark's widow: you know, the office manager from the port authorities. She used to be a parishioner of mine when I had a temporary position in Restalrig.'

'Will she be all right? She's in a terrible state.'

When the minister turned around Tod could see he too had a tear in his eye. 'Her son is down stairs in

Costa. He wouldn't come up: didn't want anything to do with a God that could let that happen to his Dad. You did hear about the murder I assume?'

'I heard about it. In fact, I spent a good part of Friday morning in Fettes with DI Sandra Laing and her colleague. They had Tracey in for questioning yesterday too but didn't tell her about the murder. I assume Mark and Jake will be next. Bob's been to see Jimmy McGuire in Saughton.'

'What in heaven's name has this got to do with Jimmy McGuire?'

'It's a long story, but it's possible he organised it. After Tracey's husband Harry was arrested for breaking in to the port offices then beaten up, Tracey went to see McGuire and told him about it. I think she may have asked for his help.'

'Well no fears there then. Jimmy really has turned a new leaf Tod and has definitely found God. There is no way on this earth he would have taken this kind of revenge, on anyone's behalf.'

'How can you be so sure? Tracey has helped him learn to read and be able to access his God through His Word, an eye for an eye and all that. Old habits die hard and just maybe he felt it necessary.'

'Are you questioning my judgement? I visited Jimmy and worked with him after his son's death. He's a changed man and you'd better get used to that.'

Callum's defence of McGuire was beginning to sound threatening, causing Tod to reflect on Bob's tale of the Special Boat Service. The visit from the office manager's wife had obviously affected him badly. 'I just find it coincidental that she visited McGuire after Harry was beaten up and less than a week later the office manager met his end.'

'Yes, but did you hear how the poor man was found? He was left gutted and displayed like a large fish in a fish market. It reminded me of the drug cartel methods in the late nineties in Columbia. Those methods came to be known as folk art. Don't you think that a wee bit extreme, under the circumstances?'

'From what I heard of Jimmy McGuire, when he was running the Fort, he was one evil man. I'm not sure what he is capable of now,' answered Tod.

'Let me remind you that there is one man in town for the moment, who is more than capable of this type of thing and witnessed it often enough in Columbia. It was that same man who gave Harry the get out of jail free card, wasn't it?' Callum stopped speaking and walked back to the window before continuing. 'Anyway, I think we'd better leave it there for now. Maybe you'd be better concentrating on looking after Tracey. If indeed she did ask Jimmy to get involved, then she is going to suffer terribly, whether he did it, or not.'

'What about you? Are you going to look after Nick Clark's family?'

'Me? If they need it. But first I've a prison visit to take care of.'

Men of the cloth are not known to lie, except in exceptional circumstances and Callum felt that need when he'd told Tod he had first to arrange a prison visit, when the first thing he was going to do was contact Peter Blue.

'Sergeant Mackie, to what do I owe the pleasure?'

Callum wasn't wearing the old boy pretence at familiarity. 'Peter, this is about me and you and I need to see you today.'

'Sorry old boy, but I'm up to my eyes in it.'

'Peter, it wasn't a request.'

Callum thought the line had gone dead when no reply was forthcoming and was about to try to redial when Peter's voice broke the silence. *'What's this about?'*

'I think you know what it's about Peter. It's about why you are here in Edinburgh. And you can dispense with the stuff about protecting Rebecca. Are you involved in the murder of port authority manager?'

'I haven't the faintest idea what you are talking about Callum. What manager, and what murder? Humour an old man for a moment and fill me in with the details.'

'Harry Cowan, the man you sprung from Constitution Street Police Station was accused of breaking into the port authority offices in the docks. It's that office manager who's been murdered, and in a way reminiscent of what we witnessed in Columbia, and what we were part of. He was sliced up like a dead fish.'

'Just a minute Callum. Do you honestly believe that I have come to your beloved city to get myself involved in a heinous crime? Why in Heaven's name would I do that? Don't you think you'd be better speaking to Harry Cowan and his companions at JP Associates. I'm sure they'll be able to shed more light on it than I can.'

Callum thought for a moment before replying. 'Peter, is this about Rebecca's involvement with JP Associates? Is this your way of repaying Bob for the exposé of the Fort fiasco and of making sure Rebecca is no longer involved with them, by putting them in the firing line and setting them up for murder? I hope for your sake it isn't. Those men and woman are worth more to this world than you and all your fancy chat and are worth more to me too. I'll not have it Peter. I've seen what you are capable of and you are certainly more than capable of what has just happened. Maybe the best thing you could do now, for everyone's sake, is to get on a plane and go back where you belong.

'Now just one-minute Sergeant Mackie, you really are stepping way over the line here. You may be right that I don't particularly warm to Bob James and his supposed colleague Tod, but I have no idea what you are talking about regarding a dead body in Leith Docks. I think it is time you remembered to whom you are addressing those accusations.'

'Oh, I remember all right, and I think it is time for you to drop the Sergeant Mackie. I am no longer your employee and no longer willing to turn a blind eye to the strange world of Peter Blue!' Callum switched off his mobile.

'Vengeance is mine sayeth the Lord,' said Peter into the void.

Callum Mackie switched his phone back on and dialled the prison.

As Callum walked slowly away from the prison, cutting between the four-in-a-block 1930s houses of Saughton Park, he reflected on a day that had begun with trying to console the wife of the deceased Nick Clark, then lecturing Tod regarding the virtues of Jimmy McGuire and had ended with his meeting the man himself. He wasn't sure if he'd been of any help to the widow, and that bothered him as much as it had in the past when he been a fully paid up Minister of the kirk and carried out pastoral visits to the bereaved. As often as not the relatives would be atheist, struggling to come to terms with death.

He hadn't had a problem arranging a meeting with Jimmy. Most of the prison staff knew him from his prison visits: although not the official prison pastor, most of the reception staff, wardens and prisoners remembered him.

What had surprised Callum was just how defensive Jimmy was when asked if he had been involved in any reprisal against those who had beaten up Harry Cowan. Jimmy hadn't answered at first and that told Callum all he needed to know, or so he thought.

When Jimmy did begin telling the story about Tracey's visit and how he had talked her out of vengeance, he began crying. Callum had never seen the man reduced to tears, not even when he'd given him the news of his son's death.

When he'd recovered, and Callum had given him his hanky to wipe his tears, Jimmy swore that he had merely instructed some acquaintances to warn the office manager to back-off.

Callum believed him but remained puzzled about who had arranged that Harry be beaten up. He couldn't for the life of him believe that the port authorities would find it necessary to carry out such a deed because of a mere burglary. Jimmy agreed, eventually, and both men were left believing that Harry's mugging was a complete coincidence and nothing at all to do with the port authority. Callum decided not to mention the death of the office manager, knowing that Bob James would have done so, during his visit and in no uncertain terms.

Before Callum left, Jimmy had asked him for a breakdown of the whole story from beginning to end and Callum had obliged and explained how he and Tod had visited the docks on the night of the Captain's birthday and how Bayani had pointed to the oil supply ship and spoke of imports that remained hidden from view.

'Dae ye ken what ship he was actually talking about?' Jimmy had asked.

Callum had assumed at the time that the direction of Bayani's wandering finger had been nothing more than conjecture as it swept the scene. McGuire questioned that idea.

'He might have been pointing at one particular boat. What if the HMV Telemachus was in dock?'

'The what?' asked Callum, before remembering where he'd heard the name before. 'That was the ship that was sold to Shifty Stewart for a few thousand pounds by her majesty's Customs and Excise, even though it was worth hundreds of thousands. It was confiscated during a drug raid, am I right? I often wondered what had happened to that boat.'

'Who knows, but maybe there is mair tae Bayani's claim than meets the eye, eh Minister.' Jimmy stood up and called for the warden, firmly putting an end to their meeting.

That man Jimmy McGuire has indeed found God, thought Callum as he stood at the bus stop on Saughton Drive, and that is a day worth celebrating. He's trying to tell me something that goes beyond honour amongst thieves, and if the man is right, then Bayani knows a lot more than we gave him credit for.

CHAPTER EIGHTEEN

Tuesday 2nd December

When the waitress popped her head around the kitchen door of the restaurant and told Mark that someone was waiting to speak to him, he assumed it was one of his friends from JP Associates. He got the shock of his life when he came out of the kitchen and saw a young man holding a police warrant card. It wasn't just the fact that the police had come calling but that this detective was the one he'd handed illegal information to at Fettes Command Centre during JP Associates last case. His only hope was that the policeman didn't recognise him.

'Is this another job you have as well of your delivery work for Yellow Pedals?' asked DS Mackay.

Mark wasn't sure whether to head back into the kitchen or try to bluff his way out of it. He opted for the second option. 'I...'

'Don't bother answering that Mark. The package which you delivered led to the conviction of some very wicked people. We wouldn't want Detective Inspector Bob James finding out it was you who delivered it, would we?' DS John Mackay could never get used to the fact that Bob James was no longer his boss.

The detective ushered Mark across to a table in the corner where a red-haired woman was sitting, going over some notes. 'This is DC Whalen,' said the DS.

The DC looked up from her notes. 'We are here to interview you in connection with the murder of Mr Nick Clark, office manager to the port authority in Leith. Please will you sit down.'

Mark had never been so frightened in his life and DC Whalen could see that.

'Mark le Mot, on the afternoon of Monday 24th November, under false pretences, you met Nick Clark, office manager to the port authority, and after extorting money from him, you arranged to meet him the following Monday. Is that correct?'

If DC Whalen thought the frightened young man facing her was going to be a walk-over she wasn't as good a reader of character as she believed.

'Excuse me if I'm wrong but are you not part of the Cold Case Squad and nothing to do with recent crime?' he asked, causing John Mackay to smile.

'What I am, and am not, is nothing to do with you, young man. My brief is concerned with bringing criminals like yourself to justice, whether for past crimes or present.' She turned her hard gaze on DS Mackay before turning back to Mark. 'Where did you get the information regarding my designation?'

'You obviously know I can read, albeit that I am merely a young man. I saw it on DS Mackay's warrant card. It reads POLICE SCOTLAND, COLD CASE UNIT'.

'Oh no, not another bloody smart-arse. Does your boss teach all his associates how to be so awkward and obstreperous?'

'My boss is through in the kitchen, you could ask him.' As he said this Mark could tell from the look on her face that he was treading on very thin ice.

DS Mackay tried a diversionary tactic. 'Do you know how serious taking money under false pretences is Mark? You could go to jail.'

'We handed the proceeds from our collection tins into Bethany; they have a literacy unit. That was the plan all along. It was literacy work we were collecting for.' At that moment Mark was very glad he'd talked Jake into handing the proceeds into Bethany. 'You can check that if you wish. We handed it in that same afternoon.'

'Would that be the "royal we" by any chance?' asked the DC.

'I think you must know by now to whom I'm referring.'

'Oh, I do. In fact, we paid him a visit at his bench prior to coming to see you and he corroborates your story. Did you know that your loyal friend has been in and out of our interview rooms more than the office cleaner Mark? His word is not exactly something you could build a defence on.' She said, before being interrupted by the younger, yet senior officer.

'We've checked with Bethany and they do corroborate your story Mark. What really interests us, and the Cold Case Squad, is your involvement with Nick Clark and your intended meeting with him. Why did you wish to have a tour of the docks and supply ships?'

'I didn't. It was the office manager who invited me to look around. We got on very well and he asked if I'd like to see the ships close up.'

'Are we expected to believe that?' DC Whalen butted in.

'What else do you expect? That I accosted him, stole his money and forced him to agree to take me round the docks. It happened just as I have said, and Jake will tell you the same thing.' Mark thought for a moment. 'How did you find out that Mr Clark had arranged to take me round the docks?'

'He'd told his office junior and he'd put it in the diary, Nigel,' answered DS Mackay as he stood up to leave, then changed his mind and leaned over the table. 'Why did you use a false name, when you were merely collecting for charity Mark?'

'We wish to keep our charity work secret from the rest of them. You know what sort of ribbing we might get.'

'Oh, I see,' said the DS, causing his DC to cough loudly.

'Is that it?' asked Mark, turning to her.

'For the moment,' replied DC Whalen, 'for the moment.'

'Oh, there is one other question,' added the DS. 'Who else knew that you'd arranged a visit to see round the ships?'

'No-one.'

'What, not even Tod?'

'No. We hadn't told anyone at JP Associates that we were going to Ocean Terminal to collect money that Monday or about my arranged meeting.'

As Mark was being interviewed, Callum was in the port offices asking if it was okay to visit the coal-supply ship and speak with the crew. The office junior chose to write the request in the diary, giving Callum the opportunity to look at the diary.

'I heard about the death of your boss,' said Callum.

'Aye,' answered the boy. 'It was terrible. There is a policeman on duty here now since it happened. Did you see him as you came in?'

'I did, yes. Anyway, I must be going. I didn't catch your name lad.'

'Steven, Steven Foley.'

'Well son, I hope you don't mind my saying, but you are not looking too well. It must have been an awful shock.'

The boy was silent for a moment before a tear broke free and ran down his cheek. 'It was all my fault.'

'What was your fault. You could not be responsible for such wickedness Steven.'

'But in a way I was. It was me who left the window unlocked: the window that the burglar used to get into the building. It was my job to make sure everything was locked up at night and I forgot that one window. If I hadn't done that then these men would not have come here and Mr Clark might still be alive.'

'Steven, there is no proof that those men had anything to do with the death of your boss and it is highly likely they did not. You cannot blame yourself for this son.' Callum pulled up a chair and sat down beside the boy. He took a packet of tissues from his pocket and handed it to him. 'I have to be going now but please believe me, you had nothing to do with this.'

'I think I did,' answered the young man, reaching for the tissues.

Before heading across the docks towards the coal ship, Callum stopped beside the policeman on duty and asked him to keep an eye on the boy, explaining that he thought that recent events were affecting him badly.

When he reached the coal ship he could see that the Captain was on the dock checking the ropes that tied his boat to the capstans. As ever, his greeting was warm, despite the freezing December wind that cut around every corner of the docks.

'And greetings to you too Joshua. It's been a wee while,' said Callum.

'It is barely a month since the party. Do you wish me to assemble the crew?'

'No, that won't be necessary. I'll catch you when you return from your next trip. Actually. it was Bayani I wanted a word with.'

'Bayani? He is no longer with us.'

'Oh, I see. The last time we met he did seem as if he could have been a little homesick. When did he leave?'

'I am not exactly sure. About one week after your last visit he just disappeared. He must have decided to jump ship. The last he was sighted was in a restaurant in Newhaven. I think he must have been homesick, as you say. It does happen.' The Captain took his gaze from Callum and looked out across the cold dock.

'Did Bayani ever discuss an oil supply ship named HMV Telemachus?' asked Callum, as his gaze followed Joshua's.

'Do you think he may have found work there? The oil ships pay better money and I know he was finding the voyages to north Russia more and more difficult.'

'No, I don't think so. It's just that he mentioned the oil supply ships last time we met.'

'Oh that. Bayani was always going on about one conspiracy or another. Did he mention those ships bringing in clandestine cargo?'

'He did, as a matter of fact.'

'You must understand, many of my crew come from tribal villages where stories of evil persist throughout their culture. I wouldn't pay too much attention to Bayani's stories. He is probably back home now listening to some story or other. As for tales about the Telemachus, I would take them with a large pinch of salt.'

'Oh, I see.' Callum walked up and shook the Captain's hand. 'Well Joshua I'd better let you get on with your work, I've held you up long enough.'

'You've not held me up at all Callum. We are grounded, so to speak. It would seem your government no longer has a need for our cargo and I am waiting instruction as to what to do with it. It may be that we dump it in the Forth then all jump ship.'

'I'd no idea Joshua. You should have phoned me.'

'I'm afraid it is out of God's hands too Mr Mackie. Myself and my crew are already sending off our CVs. We may not be around here for your Easter service.'

Callum stepped away from Joshua till he was out of earshot. Taking his mobile phone from his pocket he punched in Tod's number. 'Tod. we need to speak to Harry.'

'What's this about Callum?'

'It's about the men who beat him up. We need to be able to identify them ASAP. I wouldn't mind a word with Tracey too. Do you know where they live? It's off Crewe Road somewhere, isn't it? I'll see you outside the post-office at the bottom of the hill in one hour. And Tod, see if you can track down Bob. We may need him.'

It was obvious to Tod that this was urgent enough for him not to ask why they needed to identify Harry's assailants ASAP.

When Callum phoned, Tod had been studying Valerie's painting, which took pride of place in their office. Like most of her work it was in watercolour and depicted Newhaven Harbour and the Firth of Forth beyond. Tod prided himself on art analysis having studied Art History at Cambridge prior to choosing English Literature for his degree. He looked closely but as always Valerie's work was nearly impenetrable, almost like viewing the scene through a fine gauze. He'd been about to get a magnifying glass from the desk drawer when Callum rang.

It was almost exactly to the hour when Callum stepped off the number 14 bus outside the post-office at the bottom of Crewe Road. Tod had parked his ancient VW Polo across the street in Crewe Crescent. Both men walked up the hill towards Tracey's on opposite sides of the road from each other, without a greeting.

'What's this about then Callum?' asked Tod, when the Minister eventually came across to him.

'I think we'd be better waiting until we have all the facts before us. It may be that Harry will have something to add to the pot.'

When they reached Tracey's front door there was no sign of Bob. Tod rang the bell as Callum looked around at the converted prefabs. 'I remember these from when I was a wee boy. They were made of corrugated iron and looked more like Nissen huts.'

The door opened, and Bob stood looming over them. 'What took you so long?' He ushered them into Tracey's living room which was at the back of the house. A plate glass window looked out on one of the most beautiful tropical gardens Tod had ever seen. Tracey and Harry were sitting in adjacent armchairs either side of a real-flame fire. The three men squeezed onto the settee opposite them. It was obvious to Tod that Tracey had been crying and he hoped that this had not been Bob's doing.

Tod opened the discussion. 'Tracey, you've not been answering your phone.'

'No, we've been having problems wie the line.'

'Are you having problems with your mobile too?'

'Ye dinnae get much of a signal in here,' said Harry, ever the IT expert.

'Aye, I would agree with that,' added Bob 'You don't get much reception.'

'Nae wonder, ye come tae our door unannounced and ye expect the red carpet. The last time you were in here Bob James it was tae arrest ma Harry, and you expect tae be welcomed wie open arms. Well it's not happening!' exclaimed Tracey.

'Now there's no need to be like that Tracey,' said Tod, 'we're only here to see if there is anything we can do to help.'

Callum recognised Tod's attempt at benevolent lying and decided this was not the time.

'That's not strictly true Tracey. We need to ask Harry some questions regarding the night he was attacked.'

'And I need to ask you some questions Tracey about your visit to Jimmy McGuire and whether it instigated an action that may have led to the death of the port office manager,' said Bob.

Tracey stood up quickly and disappeared from the room almost before Bob could finish his sentence.

'Right,' said Tod, addressing Harry, when she was out of earshot, 'let's get one thing clear. I am here because I am concerned about you both. Those two clowns may have their reasons and those reasons are concerned with recent events, but I am here because I am worried about you. Would you like me to ask them to leave?' Tod stood up and turned to face the other two men.

It had been years since Bob had seen Tod so angry. He'd seen it in the past when they were growing up in Granton, but he'd forgotten that anger was still there, just under the surface. Callum had never seen this side of Tod and put his head down to avoid his gaze.

'Dinnae be daft Tod,' said Tracey, coming back into the livingroom. 'A've put the kettle on. Maybe we can all have a cuppa before Bob arrests us.'

Bob couldn't help but smile at her sarcasm while Tod merely sat down again.

Once Tracey had gone to make the tea, Harry apologised for the act that had caused so much trouble and tried to explain that Tracey had not been herself since Tod had told her about the murder.

'Why might that be do you think?' asked Bob. 'Not anything to do with her visit to McGuire, is it?'

Tod answered for Harry. 'Because the woman has been through a lot recently, or didn't you notice that detective? You forget, we are all on the same side here. You ask us to do your work for you and Sandra Laing then turn on us when things go pear-shaped.'

'She mentioned me getting beaten up to Jimmy McGuire and now she blames herself, even though A've told her it's aw ma fault.'

'Imagine her still believing that bastard McGuire has turned over a new leaf,' said Bob laughing slightly, until he remembered a Minister was present.

'He has,' said Callum. 'I can assure you of that Bob. I've spoken with him too and he has admitted to me confidentially that he did have someone speak to the staff at the offices but only to warn them the danger they'd be in if Harry was injured again and I believe him. Talk about overkill; even you can see that murder is a bit extreme in this case.'

Tracey returned from the kitchen and placed a tray of mugs and biscuits on the coffee table. 'These walls have ears and I could hear every word Bob,' she said.

'Surely you can understand why we need to ask these questions Tracey. Not one of us is immune to questioning,' Bob answered.

'Interrogation, I believe is the correct term,' said Tod.

Callum intervened hoping to prevent the coming storm. 'It was my idea to come here Tracey, not Bob's, because I believe we have to take stock of where we are. I've just discovered that the sailor who began this whole affair with his theories, has disappeared, only a month since he told us about the ships, and that worries me. What also worries me is that there could have been one ship in dock that night that carries with it a history of illegal importing. That was the Telemachus, the ship used by Shifty Stewart for his drug importing. It may have been that ship that Bayani was pointing at.'

'Well surprise, surprise,' said Bob. 'I take it you have read the Scotsman this morning.'

'A get the Sun,' answered Harry.

'The latest figures, relating to drug offences in Scotland have just been published and it would seem our festival city, apart from being awash with tourists, is awash with hard drugs.'

'Just like the good old days,' added Callum.

'Good old days or not, our esteemed leader is not happy. The Cold Case Squad has been suspended in mid-flight and we have been given the job of joining up with the drug's squad and sorting the problem. That's a laugh eh.'

Tod stood and walked over to the window. 'That's a beautiful garden you have Tracey. You never mentioned you were into gardening.'

'It's Harry's garden. A didnae mention it cause A didnae want the big polisman there sticking his neb in and talking tae Harry aw day about his pelargoniums.'

'Who told you about my…' Bob suddenly stopped and let out a loud laugh, realising that Tracey's ridicule was a sign of her recovery.

'There are no secrets in Leith, are there Tracey,' laughed Callum.

'Harry, can you not remember anything about the men who beat you up,' asked Tod, still looking out of the window.

'Not a thing. A was half-pished remember.'

'You'd gone straight to the Anchor Inn after the cafe. Did you not see anyone following you when you left there?' Bob questioned.

'No, the first thing A heard was a car door slamming shut. Then almost immediately the boots of four men were laying intae me. They must have been waiting for me in their truck.'

'Truck?' asked Bob.

'Aye,' said Harry. 'A've got a photo on ma phone.'

'You've got a photo on your bloody phone. Why did you not tell us that before?'

'After they beat me up they were walking away laughing tae themselves. A waited till they got into their truck and took ma phone out and snapped.'

'Can I see it,' asked Bob.

'Hey Babe,' Harry addressed Tracey, 'go and get that picture I printed for Bob.'

Tracey disappeared and returned with an A4 photograph of the vehicle. The windows were blacked out and it was impossible to see the faces of the men inside.

'It's a Nissan Navara Outlaw,' said Harry.

'A real man's car!' said Callum.

'A'll real man them if A get ma hands on...' Tracey stopped in mid-flow.

No-one passed any remark about vengeance and they all sat in silence for a moment.

'Did you hear them speaking?' asked Bob.

'No,' replied Harry.

'No posh voices?' asked Callum.

'You're thinking about Uncle Peter, aren't you,' commented Bob.

'Uncle Peter?' replied Callum. 'Don't you mean Peter Blue, ex MI5 operative and ex Colonel in the SAS: a man capable of carrying out much more than what we've witnessed recently.'

'For goodness sake Callum, the man is merely here because he is concerned for his niece!' Bob immediately regretted sounding so defensive.

Callum stood. 'Should we remove him from our enquiries then Bob, on the grounds that he, though capable of everything we've witnessed and the one who got Harry released from jail, is Rebecca's uncle? We wouldn't want Rebecca getting upset, now would we.'

'This has nothing to do with Rebecca!' shouted Bob, standing up.

'No, but it has everything tae dae wie me and Harry, eh Bob,' Tracey stated. 'It's funny how you can be so selective with your enquiries; once a polisman, always a polisman.'

'Listen,' said Tod. 'I think it's time we were going, to

give everybody a chance to cool down a little. Tracey are you coming into work tomorrow? We can discuss it more then.'

'A'll see,' Tracey replied, which told Tod that she would be.

As the three men were stepping out across the threshold Callum suddenly asked them to wait a moment and disappeared back into the living room. 'Harry, what are you not telling us?'

'A cannae tell ye.'

'Why not?'

'A'd never live it down.'

'Harry, do you realise that without knowing who it was, suspicion is rife, and it implicates Tracey.'

Harry thought for a moment. They were wearing high-viz vests.'

'And what else?'

'You must promise never tae tell anybody.'

'It's a promise. Now who was it?'

'The men whae beat me up, they were...No, you'll need tae go, A cannae tell ye.'

CHAPTER NINETEEN

Wednesday 3rd December

Callum spent a restless night before coming to a decision. When he phoned, Peter Blue was just being dropped off at Bruntsfield Golf Course by Rebecca. She'd suggested he meet an old accountant friend of hers, the one who dealt with the Edinburgh end of her property portfolio. Peter had met him once at Newmarket, where they both stabled horses. He was looking forward to their reunion.

'I'm sorry Sergeant Mackie but I have a lunch appointment in exactly one minute.'

'What time will you be free?'

'Impossible to say, it will depend as to whether Andrew still takes a wee dram, or two.'

'Peter, I need to know if you are involved, in any way, with the assault on Harry Cowan?'

'Now why in heaven's name would I want to hurt Harry? If you remember it was me who got him released from Constitution Street police station.'

'Exactly. How did you find out he was there in the first place?'

'Now now Callum, think about it. Harry is given one phone call to make and not knowing what else to do, he

phoned Tracey and Tracey phoned Rebecca because she didn't want to involve her beloved Tod. And who did Rebecca phone? Her uncle, of course. No conspiracy and no intrigue. I was merely helping a friend of Rebecca's. Now I'm sorry but I really do have to go, or my friend will not be best pleased.

Tracey did turn up for work that afternoon and it was she who took the call from Bob.

'Oh Tracey, glad you made it in. Are you feeling a bit better?'

'Aye, but nae thanks tae you. A thought ye were gonnae arrest me yesterday!'

'Now don't start that again. Is Tod there?'

'Aye, A'll just get him.'

'No don't bother, just tell him to meet me at the Starbank at five.' Bob hung up before Tracey could come up with a jibe.

'Boss, ye'll have tae cancel Valerie for tonight. That was our esteemed leader and he wants ye tae meet him in the Starbank at five.'

'Oh, bloody hell!' called Tod from the kitchen.

When Tod arrived, Bob and Callum were already seated by the window and were enjoying a dram. He was getting tired and hoped the two men were sharing stories from their gardens. That might save him from another round of conspiracy theories. Unfortunately, he could see from the look on their faces that gardens were not on the agenda. He ordered a pint of real ale and walked up to the table.

'I was just telling Callum that our Sandra Laing is in her element,' said Bob.

'Why is that?' asked Tod.

'Why wouldn't she be, she's heading up the new drug-busting team and been given the lead role in Project Aunt Nora.'

'Project Aunt Nora?' asked Tod.

'It's one of the many street names for cocaine,' answered Callum. 'I'd have thought you'd know that from your experience in North Telford.'

'So did I,' said Bob, half-smiling.

Tod knew that Bob was referring to Tod's arrest for receiving drugs prior to being removed from that job in North Telford. He wasn't sure about Callum's reference. He sat down with his back to the window.

'I've been stood down as consultant, now that the Cauld Case Squad has been disbanded,' said Bob.'

'Is that why you phoned?' asked Tod.

'In part. You know that my consultancy fee helps fund your and Mark's olive addiction.'

'I thought you'd taken care of that with Rebecca's funding?'

'She is certainly part of your business,' added Callum. 'It was Rebecca who was responsible for getting Harry released from jail.'

Tod swallowed his pint. 'Listen, would you gents mind if I let you carry on with this. I've an appointment at five o'clock.' He looked at his watch.

'Valerie?' asked Callum.

Tod didn't bother to reply.

'If you remember partner, it's because of you that we are involved in this case,' said Bob, standing up to get the drinks in.'

'He is right Tod,' said Callum as Bob walked away.

'If you remember Callum, I'm the one who has being trying to dump the case.'

'I think we're well past that now, don't you? Remember, Bayani, the sailor who told you about illegal imports, has disappeared. The crew believe he had jumped ship but I'm not so sure. We'd better wait till

Bob comes back and discuss the whole issue.'

Bob laid three large drams on the table and took his seat once more.

'I was hoping this wasn't going to take too long,' said Tod.

'It will take as long as it takes Tod,' replied Bob.

'Right, if we could just lay our differences aside for the moment,' Callum interceded. 'Tod you'll get to see Valerie, but we need to iron this out first.'

Tod knew from what Valerie had told him about the Fort project and meeting Callum, that Callum was jealous of his relationship with Valerie but he was keeping that to himself.

'Let's, for the sake of sanity, forget all conspiracy theories,' Bob looked at Tod as he said this, 'and go back to the beginning and see what we are up against. We don't have a case as such, so let's just talk things through and see where we are. Firstly, back at the beginning of November Tod was given an insight into the possibility that illegal imports may be entering Edinburgh via the off-shore supply vessels docked in Leith. This coincided with the Cauld Case Squad being asked to look into the William Stewart file. William, or Shifty Stewart as he was known, was responsible for importing drugs into Edinburgh before his incarceration and subsequent death. Stewart was known for using off-shore vessels and had actually purchased one, the Telemachus for a knock-down price. even though the ship was worth at least £500,000. Then there is the mystery of Stewart's death, which led Police Scotland to decide to reopen that case. It's only hearsay but many believe MI5 may have been involved in his death.'

'I thought you'd been asked to stand down from that case?' said Tod.

'Don't interrupt my train of thought,' snapped Bob, sharply. 'Then Harry, trying to guarantee that Tracey remained in a job with JP Associates, did you the service of breaking into the port offices and was caught. Then Peter Blue, Rebecca's uncle, appeared suddenly and got him released. Then...'

Both Tod and Callum interrupted Bob, simultaneously, Tod getting in first. 'Harry wasn't doing me any favours Bob, I knew nothing about the break in until he'd been caught, and you know that.'

Callum spoke up next. 'Uncle Peter never appears out of the blue. Uncle Peter has never done a spontaneous thing in his life and whatever he is in Edinburgh for, I am convinced it is not merely looking after his beloved niece. It would not surprise me if he is involved in some way in the Stewart investigation and...'

It was Bob's turn to interrupt. 'Right, both of you, I began by saying we could leave conspiracy theory aside for the moment. We are only interested in hard facts!

Then our Tracey visited McGuire in Saughton and told him about Harry being assaulted and the next thing we knew, two heavies visited the dock office and threatened the young lad there.' Bob took a large quaff of his whisky before continuing. 'Then guess what, low and behold two of our associates, namely, Jake Robinson and Mark le Mot, met the dock office manager and arranged for Mark to visit his office and have a tour of the ships. Some days after that arrangement the manager was found dead. That's where we are at the moment boys, up to our necks in it!'

As Bob leaned back against his chair the barman laid three more whiskies on their table. 'They're from the gentleman at the bar.' He pointed to Sandy Grassick, who was leaning, one arm on the bar, and smiling over at them.

Callum waved him over. 'Sandy, this is becoming a habit. I've certainly seen you in here more recently than in the kirk.'

'Aye this became my new haunt Minister. I've heard more sense from this pulpit here,' he ran his hand along the bar. What brings you gentlemen out on a wicked night like this?'

'Bob here was just filling us in on our investigations so far,' said Callum.

'Aye, and I'd have been as well talking to the wall

Sandy,' replied Bob.

'Oh, I don't know about that Bob, half the folk at the bar were listening, including me and if you don't mind me saying so, I may have an idea myself. I've never been one to shy away from a good tale.'

'Here we go again, another bloody conspiracy theorist,' whispered Bob.

'This is no theory,' said Sandy,' walking over to their table. It picks up on where you left off a moment ago. In fact, if Mark le, whatever his name is, managed to get himself an invitation to look around the off-shore vessels then the lad has gumption. Tell me, how else would you get to know the ins and outs of their dealings. If I were you, I'd try to arrange for Mark to make that visit.'

'You're a man after my own heart Sandy,' said Callum, 'and I could go with him. In fact, he's much more likely to gain access if the Pastor to seamen is with him.'

'And what do you think you'll find there?' asked Bob. 'Are you thinking that their holds will be full of smack and the crew will just hold up their hands and surrender? Personally, I think it is a complete waste of time.'

'Do you have any better ideas?' asked Tod.

'Maybe. First and foremost, I'm going to have a word with Peter Blue and try to ascertain exactly why he is up here. What about you partner, you're used to finding the way forward, have you any ideas?'

'My main priority is looking after Tracey, and Harry for that matter. I am worried about them both and not least because Harry has not recovered from that beating and Tracey is struggling with the fact she mentioned it to McGuire.' When Tod decided benevolent lying was the way forward he could be very convincing.

'Would that be Jimmy McGuire?' asked Sandy.

'You know him then?' asked Bob.

'We had a run in when he and his tribe tried to muscle in on my wee fishing trips. He even suggested he could use my wee boat for other, more lucrative cargo.'

'Did you know he found God in prison?' asked Callum.

'I did actually. Mind you, stranger things have happened. Listen gents, I've got to be going but if you intrepid sleuths ever need a wee boat trip I would be more than happy to help.'

'Is that you trying to muscle in on our patch?' said Callum.

'You know how I feel about those people that bring

such misery to our streets.' At that Sandy was gone.

After explaining that JP Associates could do a lot worse than have Sandy Grassick on board, Callum announced his departure too.

CHAPTER TWENTY

Thursday 4th December

Bob, always the early riser, thought it prudent to arrive at Rebecca's without notice. It was only just gone eight o'clock and Gamekeepers Road was deserted, apart from the commuters making their way in and out of town in cars. When he rang the bell, he expected her to be dressed in night attire and slippers. She was fully dressed.

'Bob, to what do I owe the pleasure at this time of a morning? Up with the larks, as ever. You'd better come in, but I must warn you I have a visitor.'

Bob's heart sank at the thought that Rebecca may have found someone else and he'd stayed the night. 'No, listen Beccy, if it's not convenient I can come back another time.'

'It is convenient actually, we were just talking about you. He knows you, and I've just made some coffee. Come through, he's in the conservatory.'

When Bob walked into the large, well heated, garden-room Uncle Peter was sitting at the far end on a Chesterfield settee. He stood up and put out his hand. 'Well talk of the devil, or Police Scotland, depending on which way one looks at it. Good to see you again Bob.' They shook hands. 'Are you always appearing at people's doors at this time in the morning or is that practice reserved for my niece only?'

'I'm pleased to see you too Peter,' said Bob, sitting down beside him. 'In fact, I'd only come along to ask Bec...Rebecca where I might find you.'

'I'm staying in the Balmoral. We sat up into the early hours this morning, so I took to Rebecca's spare room. I've got to say your fair city is making me most welcome.' At that moment Rebecca came in carrying a tray of scones and large cafetière. 'Bob has always had perfect timing Uncle. He can smell strong coffee and cheese scones a mile off.'

'Actually darling,' said Peter, 'I wouldn't have minded a quick word with Bob, if that's okay?'

'Oh, I see, the gentlemen's club again.' Rebecca put down the tray, turned and left the room without another word.

'She is a good girl Bob and I would do anything for her.'

'Including interfering in our investigations and causing us enough grief as to encourage her not to have anything to do with JP Associates?'

'You don't happen to have been speaking with Sergeant Callum Mackie by any chance?'

'As a matter of fact I have, and from what he tells me, you are more than capable of carrying out any action that will get you whatever you want.'

'Tell me the truth Bob, do you honestly believe that I would attempt to interfere in your plans for JP Associates? I care deeply about my niece and believe it or not, I happen to know that working with your agency makes her very happy, and I am not going to spoil that, particularly on the back of Sophie's disappearance.'

Bob was taken aback for an instant then remembered what Callum had said Peter was capable of. 'Is your being here in Edinburgh anything to do with the MI5 cover up relating to Shifty Stewart and the Telemachus? That happened on your watch, didn't it?'

'Don't tell me that little problem has raised its head again. Are you involved in the case? Has the Cold Case Unit been charged with finding the truth?'

'I was, but we've been pulled off and I've been put out to pasture, albeit temporarily, or so they say. I just find it all very coincidental that the Stewart case comes to light again and who should appear but yours truly, Peter Blue.' Bob leaned over for a scone.

Peter stood up and wandered over to look through the window to the garden. 'Do you know much about flowers Bob?'

'A little, why?'

'My wife, Wilhelmina was a great lover of roses.

That's who Rebecca takes her love and skills from. She was such a dear; she even had a rose named after her.'

'I think I remember Rebecca mentioning that.' Bob remembered the day very clearly when Rebecca had told him about her love of gardening and her Aunt Wilhelmina. He'd merely forgotten that Peter was her husband.'

'Anyway, my history is not one that I wish to revisit Bob. It is certainly not one I'm particularly proud of, but it was my life and things had to be done for Queen and Country and all that. It doesn't make me Moriarty and does not mean that everything I do is tainted by conspiracy. You do not have to believe me, but I am in Edinburgh to look after my niece's best interests. I hope you and I may get to know each other a little better while I'm here.'

'What about the Fort case? You know it was me who phoned the newspaper,' said Bob.

'I didn't know exactly, but I would have put money on it that it was you. Thank you for telling me now.'

'It wasn't personal Peter. I couldn't bear the thought that your security services were attempting to interfere in our politics.'

'It had happened before in 1707 when England was attempting to form a union with Scotland and it could have happened again if that union had been threatened. Did you know that Daniel Defoe was an English spy engaged in trying to convince the population to vote for the union?'

'Tod enlightened me to that fact. But Rebecca told me you were born in Scotland Peter, in Perthshire. So tell me, what is this with our spies; is being in London so all-consuming that they forget their past completely?'

'Something like that. When you work for Her Majesty's Security Services there is a need for a certain Englishness. You don't believe that Sean Connery would really have got the job, do you?' Peter turned from the window.

'Anyway, you're home now Peter.'

'Actually, that's what Rebecca and I were speaking about last night. She would like me to move up here and has offered to put me up until I can find myself a little pied-a-terre and I've agreed. In fact, I was wondering if you might like to help me in searching for the right property. Rebecca has offered, as she has a property portfolio and experience of this sort of thing, but I'm not in the business of using family favours and I'm not sure if the feminine touch is exactly what I'm looking for at my age.'

'So, you've no hard feelings about me having gone to the press? And what about Rebecca and me; are you happy about that?'

'Believe what you like Bob. I am telling you the truth. I hope that you and my niece do make it and I only found out about Harry from Rebecca and merely intervened on his behalf for her. I've retired from the service, though I must say it would be nice to be able to help JP Associates in some way, if I was ever needed. I've got a lot of experience in investigation and spying for that matter. It could come in handy at times.'

A scene flashed across Bob's mind of a future team meeting in the office in Leith: himself, Tod, Tracey with her notepad, Rebecca, Callum, Mark, Jake Robinson, Harry and Peter Blue. He shook his head. 'I'm sorry Peter, but I'm struggling to get my head round this.'

'Oh, and there is one other thing,' added Peter. 'I have a job for your agency. I want you to find Sophie, no matter what it costs. Her disappearance is tearing my niece apart. Will you do that for me?'

'I would have thought someone with your contacts could do that better than we can,' answered Bob, but before Peter could reply Rebecca came back in to the conservatory and lifted the cafetière. 'I'll just freshen this up. Are you old boys okay? Would you like anything else?'

Bob thought of asking her for a dram or getting her to call St. John's ambulance service as he felt he was about to pass out. The last thing he'd expected when he arrived was that he'd have a new friendship, a new associate for JP and a willing acceptance of his relationship with Rebecca. 'No, I'm fine Beccy, in fact I have to be going.'

'Do call again soon please darling,' she said, putting her arm through his and escorting him to the door.

Bob looked back at Peter whose wink merely added to his broad smile. Bob suddenly felt as if he had been a victim in another conspiracy, albeit one with a satisfactory ending.

Tod's intended victim of the day was not so easy to find. He walked the length of Princes Street Gardens twice but still no sign. Eventually he approached a young woman sitting in a sleeping bag below Scott's monument. For one moment he thought he knew her. 'Excuse me, I wonder if you could help me please. I'm looking for someone who is on...; he's tall, bearded and speaks with an English accent.'

'You mean "on the streets". That kind of information will cost you.'

Tod removed a fiver from his wallet and handed it to her.

'That widnae buy me a coffee and scone near here. A'm looking for the same amount as you'll spend the day on your breakfast, lunch, tea and drink. Surely that's no too much tae ask?'

The girl's direct approach caused Tod to reflect on his culinary plans for the day and his planned session at the Shore Bar that evening with Valerie. He handed over two twenties and his last fiver.

'Having a quiet day then,' said the girl, putting the money inside her clothing. 'Ye'll find him down in the railway station. He sits at the bottom of the slope, the perfect spot tae make a few bob fae the commuters.'

Tod walked the two hundred yards to the spot described by the girl and saw, as he walked down the slope that his money had been well spent. He was about to approach Daniel, who was sitting in a sleeping bag with his back to the parapet, but a commuter beat him to it. He expected to see the man drop something in the hat lying on the ground but instead saw him lift his finger and begin pointing at Daniel. In a split-second Daniel had the man by the finger and was pulling him down until their noses touched.

'Now, now Daniel, no need to get over excited on this fine morning,' said Tod, producing his JP business card and flashing it quickly across the other man's face. 'Police. Now fuck-off, before I let Daniel lose on you.'

Tod sat down on the pavement and leaned back against the freezing Victorian parapet.

Both men watched the pin-striped commuter make his

way to the newspaper stand in the centre of the station.

'Never use my name in public again Tod.'

'Oh Daniel, I am so sorry. I got caught up in the heat of the moment. I really am sorry.'

Daniel laughed. 'I'm not sure that gentleman will have taken the time to remember much about me though, do you? He'll more than likely remember you though,'

Tod could feel the cold from the pavement and the parapet seep through his clothes. 'Listen, I'm just going to go over to the kiosk there and get us a coffee.' He stood and removed his wallet. 'Oh shit, I gave that girl my last fiver. I couldn't borrow a fiver Dan...oops, sorry.'

'That wasn't Walter Scott's Guinevere was it. She must have felt sorry for you; she takes cheques as well.'

'That's not her real name is it?'

'No, it's Janet. She adopted Guinevere's name from Walter Scott's poem, except in her case the lady of the lake gets rained on day after day. She was studying to be an archaeologist, but the pressure got to her and she gave up uni and left her family home.' Daniel handed Tod a fiver. 'It's going to look great you taking money from a vagrant, especially if that business gent sees you, he'll think you're a copper on the make.'

When Tod returned with the coffees Daniel was

lifting his belongings and stuffing them into an old khaki coloured rucksack. 'Come-on we'll go out into the cold light of day. We might even pay Janet a visit.'

Tod suddenly began to worry that he'd put the girl in danger by asking her the whereabouts of Daniel. He decided not to broach the subject but wait things out. When they arrived at the Scott Monument the first thing Daniel did was lean over and hand Janet his coffee. 'I'm on a clean food trip now and coffee is off the list,' he said.

'I've heard about that diet,' said Janet. 'Disease only exists within us, as God's world is free from corruption so if you eat enough lettuce and pure veg juice you can purge all disease. Brilliant!'

Daniel let out a loud laugh. 'Mm, a world without corruption, now wouldn't that be nice.' He looked at Tod before putting his hand in his pocket and producing a state of the art smart- phone. He handed it to the young woman. 'I thought this might come in handy.'

'Very nice,' said the girl. 'I'll need to have it wiped.'

'I know someone who could do that for you,' broke in Tod, thinking that it might just be the very thing to distract Harry from his recent worries.

'Who is this?' Janet pointed at Tod. 'He came here earlier looking for you and I see he found you.'

'It's maybe not such a good idea to give information about where I am though.'

'Sorry Daniel. I wouldn't have if he hadn't offered me his daily ration allowance.'

Daniel laughed again before continuing. 'Next time someone asks for me just say you've never seen me and I'll give you my ration; I'm not using it just now due to my clean diet.'

The two men walked away from Janet and sat at a bench further along the garden.

'Did you take that smart-phone from the man who was giving you grief?' asked Tod.

'Smart-phone, but not such a smart gentleman,' answered Daniel.

'What's with this clean food diet? I've never heard such nonsense.'

'Neither had I. I was reading about it in a health mag I found in one of the station waste bins. Janet doesn't take kindly to charity from her peers, so I was merely covering my tracks. Tell me Tod, why are you here?'

'It's two things really. Well maybe three, but's that's more personal. The first thing I wanted to tell you was that your old boss, Peter Blue is in town. He is visiting his niece Rebecca, or so the story goes. The second thing is that JP Associates might need your help in a case that...'

Daniel interrupted. 'Does your agency know of my existence?'

'No, but you could liaise with me and I could feed back any information you may find.'

'What's the third thing?'

'It's none of my business really, but your son Toby is giving Valerie an awful lot of grief. He's talking about abandoning his studies at Aberdeen and she is running after him like a skivvy.'

'So you are still seeing Valerie, and Toby is getting in the way. I've heard about this kind of thing, when a widow meets a new boyfriend and her children don't like it.' Daniel wasn't smiling.

'It's nothing like that. Valerie is trying to hold down a good job and is really getting her life in order but that lazy bastard is holding her back.'

'And what am I supposed to do about it? I don't exist, remember.'

'Actually, I was hoping you might be able to give me some tips on how I should approach the problem. I want to help her.'

'If you don't mind me saying Tod, this is beginning to sound like a scene from a DH Lawrence novel, maybe

Sons and Lovers.'

'Listen Daniel, can we change the subject? Toby is not the main reason I came to see you. JP Associates have hit a real brick wall in an investigation. The original crime took place when you were active in Edinburgh in the nineteen-nineties. I hoped you might be able to shed some light on it.' Then he told Daniel the whole story from start to finish, including the involvement of William Stewart.

'His name did come up at team meetings at the time. In fact, I might go as far as to say we did have some sort of relationship with the said Stewart,' replied Daniel after giving Tod's tale some thought.

'That's what the police and media were reported to believe at the time of Stewart's death and that's why I'm asking for your help. You were working for MI5 in Edinburgh at the same time that Stewart and his crew were active, and I was hoping you'd have had first-hand information on his links to the security services.'

'But you already know why I was in Edinburgh: trying to scupper your devolved parliament was a completely different case from Stewart and his drug-smuggling escapades. We always worked on a need-to-know basis only for our own protection, as you can well imagine. What about asking Peter Blue? He is Rebecca's uncle and she is working with you so surely, he's your man. He was our director at the time and he will definitely have information on whether Stewart was an MI5 or Customs informant.'

'We're not sure whose side Peter is on. Rebecca seems to have great belief in her uncle but one of our associates, Callum Mackie, has warned us about Uncle Peter and what he is actually capable of, so we are treading very carefully.'

'That's no bad thing where Peter is concerned Tod, I'll give you that, but how did you manage to get yourself involved with the Reverend Mackie?'

'He was the one who took me to the coal-boat. Do you know him then?'

'Oh, I know Callum, but by name and sight only. He took, what shall we say, a strong liking to Valerie a year or two ago and as an interested party I made it my business to find out all about him. Talk about the pot calling the kettle black; when he tells you how dangerous Peter is, I think you should be aware that Callum Mackie is perhaps even more so. I do believe he did turn over a new leaf though. His ministry is no façade, as far as I can ascertain.' Daniel thought for a moment and changed the subject. 'About Toby Tod, don't you think you could have a word with him?'

The change of subject caught Tod off-guard. 'I don't feel I know Valerie well enough yet and I'm not sure Toby would take too kindly to my interference.'

'Can you blame him? Anyway, from what I hear you are more than capable of sorting this out. You are trained in conflict resolution I believe and somewhat more forceful approaches when required?'

'What do you mean, forceful approaches?'

'Remember I told you that when you started dating Valerie I did my research. Well it happened to lead me to Newcastle and to someone by the name of Jack Gould, I believe he worked with you on a case. He had a thing or two to say about your abilities.'

Tod stood up and was about to question Daniel further when he realised he might just dig the hole he'd made for himself even deeper. 'I'll be in touch. Thanks for the advice Daniel,' he said as he walked away.

Tod didn't meet Valerie that night, using feigned exhaustion as his excuse. He chose instead a visit to the local off-license and the purchase of a litre of whisky. Once ensconced in his small Victorian ground-floor flat he proceeded to rebuild the relationship he'd had with the bottle for many years when troubling thoughts became too much to bear. But his relationship with the bottle, from that bygone era, no longer worked and on that Friday night, it wouldn't play ball.

After throwing back the first whisky, he went to the kitchen drawer and took out the screwdriver, the tool that would gain him access through the floorboards to the shallow area below, and the journal he'd stored there for more than a year.

Before writing down his feelings on a new page, he reread what he'd had written after he'd murdered Richard Stark and Brian Hopper. As he read he began to realise how much things had changed since then and how much he'd changed too. He questioned his behaviour less now, and the nightmares he'd described in the journal occurred less frequently. He felt such a sense of relief that he almost closed the book and the whisky bottle, but no sooner had the thought crossed his mind, when the door-bell rang.

When he answered it, the last person he expected to see before him was Tracey. He stared without uttering a sound. It had begun raining and her hair was wet and clinging to her face.

'Well, are ye no gonnae let me in?'

Tod's mind immediately turned to the journal he'd left open on the kitchen table, believing that whoever was at his door could be sent packing. He knew instinctively that Tracey wouldn't be. 'You'd better come in, you're soaking. I'll get you a towel.'

As she stood in the hall rubbing the towel through her hair Tod began fidgeting.

'Ye dinnae have tae worry if you've got somebody in.

A can just get on the number 14 again.'

'No, I've no-one in. I was just thinking of having an early night, that's all,' answered Tod.

'Well A'll no keep ye. It's just there's something A need tae discuss wie you and A didnae want tae speak over the phone.'

'Could it not have waited till Monday?'

'No, it couldnae wait till Monday.' Tracey dropped the towel and marched through to the kitchen.'

'Is it about Harry?' he called, trying to prevent her reaching the kitchen.

'No, it's about Rebecca.' Tracey saw the journal lying on the table and turned it around to read it. She only just caught a glimpse of the last entry. It was dated 22nd May 2014.

Why did Bob have to mention "murderers"? He must know what I've done, he must, so why is he keeping it to himself.

'What's this?' she asked, pointing at the page.

'Oh that, it's nothing,' replied Tod.

'Nothing? It disnae look like nothing tae me. What this about murders?'

Tod was struggling for an answer and trying not to

break down completely and admit the whole thing.

'Well, what's it about?'

'It's about me Tracey. I'm writing a novel, but please don't tell anyone. These are just my rough notes.'

'You're writing a novel? What's it called?'

'I'm not sure yet but I was thinking about Justified Sinner, after Hogg's Confessions of a Justified Sinner.'

'You asked me tae read that book when ye were teaching me tae read and write, but A thought it was too auld fashioned.'

'This is an updated version.' Tod lifted his journal and closed it.

'Well if ye dinnae mind me saying so, you aught tae give it up because it's making you awfie tense looking.'

'I must admit, it does take it out of me, writing a novel. Having studied literature and written critique I still had no idea how hard the creative process would turn out to be. Anyway, why are you here? Is it about Rebecca?'

'Aye, she came to see me and Harry this afternoon. A 'm no sure if it's what she originally came about but when she saw me wie ma grandbairn Kylie she just broke down and started begging us tae help her find Sophie. Even though Harry's been ill, he's a right sucker for a woman's tears, especially when a missing bairn is the cause of those tears, and he blurted out a promise tae dae everything in his power tae help her. Rebecca said that she thought JP Associates could have done more, but you havnae so she wants me and Harry tae help her.'

'Now wait a minute Tracey. You are working for JP Associates and that would be a con...'

'Dinnae gie me conflict of interest, if that's what you were gonnae say? Harry and I have agreed tae help her. It might mean me taking some time off, if you dinnae mind? That's what A wanted tae tell ye.'

Tracey headed for the front door with Tod on her heals asking her to stay for coffee. 'No thanks' was all she said as she went out into the rain.

Once Tod had replaced his journal under the hall floor he phoned Bob and was about to tell him about Tracey's visit when Bob interrupted.

'Tod, we've got a new contract. Peter has tasked us with finding Sophie and I've said yes. I'm sorry I didn't get a chance to run it past you first.'

'It's no bother,' replied Tod, 'I'm sure Tracey and Harry and the rest of the team will be more than happy for us to take it on.'

'To be honest Tod, I don't give a shit whether they're happy or not. We're their bosses, or did you forget that, again?'

'Sorry Bob for a minute there I did. I'll see you Monday and we can discuss the way forward.'

'Aye the way forward right enough,' replied Bob, hanging up on his friend.

CHAPTER TWENTY-ONE

Sunday 7th December

'It's freezing,' said Mark, as he and Callum made their way across a cold and windy Leith docks.

'"I will honour Christmas in my heart and try to keep it all the year. I will live in the Past, the Present, and the Future. The Spirits of all Three shall strive within me. I will not shut out the lessons that they teach".'

'Oh no, not another one. So, who said it?'

'Charles Dickens of course.'

'Charles Dickens or not, I still don't understand why we have to be here on a Sunday, replied Mark. 'It's my only day off.'

'It used to be my busiest day,' replied the Minister.

'I see you're wearing your dog-collar. Are you still a going concern?'

'I am today, for this visitation. I normally stand in on Sunday services for ministers who are on holiday or off sick, but I don't have any services in the diary at the moment. That might be in part due to the kirk getting a wee bit exasperated by my somewhat non-conformist slant on scripture.'

'Interesting,' said Mark. 'I'd like to talk to you about

that sometime, as part of my PhD.'

'Aye Tod told me you were doing a PhD. He says you're a whizz kid in psychology.'

'I suspect it's Tod that's the whizz, not me. So why are you wearing your collar today?'

'We have come here on a Sunday because the port offices are closed. Also, security may be more likely to believe we are here to carry out a service for the seamen as it's a Sunday and I'm dressed for the occasion. It may also help us gain access to information from the crew of the ships; after all, everyone trusts a Minister, wouldn't you agree Mark?'

'Mm,' said Mark, 'we could discuss that too.'

Once through the security gates, after a hale fellow good morning with the guard, the two men headed past the port offices towards the ships.

'Remember Mark, you are a student of New College, in your final year, and are on placement with me in my role as pastor to seafarers.'

'Mm,' said Mark. 'Is that the "benevolent lying", I've heard so much about since becoming a JP associate?'

As it was a Sunday, there were not many crew members around the ships. There was however one very enthusiastic lady coming down the gangplank of the nearest one and she called out to Callum. 'I'm getting off just in time then Minister!'

'Mandy, imagine seeing you here, on a Sunday too. I thought even in your profession you took a day off. It is our Lord's day after all.'

'Needs must Callum,' she said as she approached and gave him a huge hug. There are men in there requiring my services.' She pointed up at the ship which loomed over them.

'And that will be you on your way to the Central Bar for a much-needed refreshment?'

'Aye, just the ticket on a cold Sunday morning. Sorry I can't wait around to hear your sermon.' Mandy laughed out loud.

'Before you go though, have you ever heard of a deep-sea supply ship, the Telemachus?'

'HMV Telemachus, I have that, but not in a long while. Isn't she docked at Methil now? There was talk of her being scrapped a while back.'

'Thanks Mandy, I'll not keep you from your drink and debauchery any longer.

'You didn't introduce me to your handsome friend here.' Mandy tweaked Mark's cheek, causing him to flush brightly.

'This is Mark. He is on placement with me here in Leith,' said Callum.

'Hello Mark,' said Mandy, 'That's a fine name for your chosen profession. Now see you keep a wee eye on that mentor of yours. He has a tendency to make men disappear. Isn't that right Minister? In fact, when the crew saw you coming along the dock they began disappearing down into the bilges of the ship. Anyway, must fly, a pint of eighty-shilling ale awaits.'

Mark waited till Mandy was out of sight. 'Is she, is she a pr...?'

Callum laughed out loud. 'Aye, she is that son, a professional indeed. She's First Mate on that monster up there and is studying for her Captains' ticket.'

Mark almost staggered back into the narrow strip of sea between the ship and dockside but said no more.

CHAPTER TWENTY-TWO

Monday 8th December

Tod was in the office very early. This was due in part to his desperate need to study the paperwork relating to Bayani's theory, but mostly because he'd hardly slept the whole weekend and needed to get out of the house to find distraction.

Great Junction Street was quiet as he made his way by bus to the office. He'd half hoped to see Jake on his bench, but it was even too early for him and the end of the Kirkgate was deserted. Once Tod was ensconced at the computer with a large coffee by his side he typed "HMV Telemachus" into the search box. At the same moment the office door opened, causing him in an instant to minimise the screen.

'Well talk about the early bird. A couldnae believe it when A saw ye getting off the number 7.' It was Jake.

'Talk about me, what about you, the street cleaners have not even had time to wash your bench yet.'

'Anyway, ye can maximise your screen again. Is there mair coffee in that pot?'

'There is, and it's good to see you Jake. Though I thought you preferred a takeaway coffee in the morning, compliments of Mark of course.'

'Aye, he'll be over in a wee while wie the coffees. He

kens we're here, and he's bringing one for Callum tae.'

'I don't understand?'

'Mark came to see me at the bowling club yesterday afternoon. He went with Callum to look round the supply ships yesterday and from what he told me I'd say they've got things they want tae talk about.'

'Am I always the last to find out what's going? Apart from you lot doing exactly as you please, now I've got Tracey and Harry working for Rebecca on their own account.'

'A thought ye were a believer in grass-roots democracy and aw that?'

'There's democracy and there's being taken over, and I believe I'm suffering from the latter.'

'A'll go and pour that coffee.'

Callum arrived just after nine o'clock. He was carrying a paper bag.

'Is that what I think it is?' asked Jake.

'It is Mr Robinson. Would you care to partake of a sausage roll or is a Scotch pie more to your liking?'

'Jake has been known to mix and match and partake of both, if my memory serves me well,' said Tod, just as

Mark opened the office door.

'I'm sorry, I haven't brought the coffees. It was hard enough to organise an hour off without asking for a carry-out,' he said.

Once the four men were sitting round the coffee table with their office-made brew and Greggs bakes, Tod opened the proceedings.

'First of all, let me welcome you to the offices of JP Associates. As you may be aware, I'm one of the proprietors, Thomas Peterson.'

Jake tried to interrupt but Tod continued. 'Recently, it has come to my attention that a great many of our associates have been taking things into their own hands, such as running enquiries and investigations without prior consultation of any kind with the proprietors. Wouldn't you agree?'

'It's not quite like that Tod,' replied Callum. 'We were led to believe that you were the type of leader who preferred to see his associates work on their own initiative.'

'There's "own initiative" and there is downright disregard for my authority Callum, and I think you know which one we are dealing with here. After my last run in with this lot,' he pointed around the table, 'I was made aware that I did not involve them enough. Since then I've made many changes and where has that got me;

my associates have completely taken the helm.'

'I'm glad you raised that,' answered Callum.

'So am I,' said Mark.

'Aye, so am A, for that matter,' said Jake.

'It's at the helm of a rusting deep-sea supply ship over in Fife, Methil to be exact that I believe our fortunes lie. The Telemachus is still afloat, if only just, and we need to get over there to see it,' said Callum.

'And what have we to gain by doing that?' asked Tod.

'We got so many stories on the docks yesterday about the Telemachus, varying for the mundane to the outrageous but most of the people we spoke to had heard of it and some appeared to wish they hadn't,' said Mark.

'I still don't see how looking at a rusting hulk, albeit one that was used in drug crime in the nineteen-nineties, can possibly help us in our search for the people responsible for flooding the streets of Edinburgh with drugs,' insisted Tod.

'It couldnae dae any harm, could it?' said Jake.

Before agreeing to visit Methil, Tod quizzed Callum and Mark further on their visit to the docks. Having never been aboard a deep-sea supply ship, he discovered that their holds have the capacity to carry a great many tonnes of equipment, most of it destined for the oil industry. He also discovered that there were many areas of the ships which could be used for contraband, being almost inaccessible to anyone above the weight of eight stones. The investigators had learned from one crew member that there was indeed contact with Petrobras in Brazil and certain members of the ship's company had visited Brazil as advisors to Petrobras.

No matter how convincing the stories, Tod remained sure that this was mere coincidence and had nothing whatsoever to do with drug smuggling.

'A thought ye were famed for your conspiracy theories Tod,' commented Jake, once Tod had finished his summing up and the associates were getting ready to leave the office. 'now all of a sudden you've turned intae a cynic.'

As they closed the door, leaving Tod alone, he turned once more to his computer and his search for Telemachus. It was only the early arrival of Tracey that woke him from his reveries.

'A hope you're not writing that novel in work's time,' she said as she removed her coat. 'A've been thinking; you could dae wie somebody like me in your book: somebody that speaks Scottish and has a lot of common-sense.'

'I'll be holding interviews for possible characters later

in the year and will keep you in mind,' replied Tod.

'Talking of murder, A could murder a cup of coffee. Dae ye want one?'

'Actually, I was just about to go out but wanted to see you before I go.' Tod produced the smart phone given to him by the girl below the Scott Monument and handed it to Tracey. 'Could you ask Harry if he could wipe this clean for me?'

'A don't believe this. Have ye started stealing phones now?'

'Don't be daft, I was given it by a friend who keeps up with the latest trend in phones and he passed his old one to me.'

'It disnae look auld tae me, it's a state of the art phone this one.' Tracey turned the phone around and studied it before switching it on. 'John Thomas, A've never heard of him. You never mentioned him before.' She flashed the contact information screen at Tod.

'We don't see each other much. He only appears once in a blue moon.'

'When he's got a top or the range smart phone tae give you. Interesting. A'll ask Harry tae look at it. It might be just be what he needs.'

Once Tod had left the office he phoned Bob to arrange a meeting for that afternoon. Bob was at home in Portobello and had just finished pruning his pelargoniums. *'Why don't you come down here, it's been a long time since you've set foot in the place,'* suggested Bob.

Tod was inwardly delighted to be given the invitation. 'I'll need to nip home for the car.'

'You call that old beat-up, faded-pink VW Polo a car? Anyway I'll see you when you get here. Oh, and Tod, get us a bag of mini-doughnuts on your way.'

After Bob put down the phone he began thinking about his friend and the situation that had lost him his job and left him very short of money. Bob's mind flitted across the months which saw them starting their own investigation agency and the lack of funds that had caused. If it hadn't been for Beccy's intervention, the business would not be a going concern, he was sure of that. As his mind wandered from their funding situation, it fixed once more on Tod's old car. It was at that moment he remembered finding the faded-pink piece of rusting metal on the building site adjacent to the house where Stark was murdered. The retired Detective Inspector thought hard for a moment before shaking his head and dismissing the thought.

Tod arrived within the hour. The last time he'd been in

Bob's house, his friend had not long moved and seemed happy enough living out of cardboard boxes. His kitchen was a cheap, plastic design back then, but not anymore. The backyard had been strewn with debris from a botched renovation carried out by the previous owners and looked more like Granton dump.

Bob had moved here not long after his spouse had given him his marching orders because he didn't want children. Whilst Doreen wanted a full nursery, Bob wanted a career. Doreen had gone on to have three kids to a husband who beat her continually until she'd had to escape to a women's refuge, while her man spent a long time in the infirmary, thanks to Doreen's ex-husband. Some people said it was that which prevented Bob from reaching the top of his game, even though his victim never pressed charges.

'It's through here,' said Bob as he ushered Tod through the natural wood and marble kitchen into the conservatory. If Tod was speechless on his previous visit, he was even more so now. Now he saw an Italian tiled floor and English oak woodwork, and the whole room was filled with flowers. Each window sill displayed a bloom of red pelargoniums. Tod had only come close to such quality in home-style magazines in his dentist's waiting-room.

'Before you say a word, it's my hobby. Rebecca has been helping me with ideas; she's great with the home and garden, you should know, you've seen her house.'

As he said this Bob thought about Uncle Peter and how he'd kept Rebecca at length when it came to organising his home life.

'Are these geraniums?' was all Tod could think to say as he looked around the conservatory.

'Pelargoniums. That's the botanical name. Geranium is the common name and it is more correct to use it for the garden variety.'

'Excuse me for asking,' said Tod. 'I've got to say, I am impressed.' He walked over to the window. 'Your patio has changed somewhat since I was last here too. What's the large polished stone in the corner?'

'That's a water-feature. It was Rebecca's idea too.' Bob immediately thought a change of subject in order. 'Right time for a brew; I've got one of those expresso machines if you fancy a nice coffee?'

'Was that Rebecca's idea as well? Better make mine a dram.' Tod was beginning to show the old signs of jealousy he'd felt when Bob and Rebecca had become an item.

'The drams can wait. In fact, I was going to ask you if you'd like to stay for dinner. I thought we could pop down to the local boozer for one or two then come back here?'

'Don't tell me you've started cooking now as well. I'm

beginning to wonder if the Martians have taken you away and replaced you with a new version of yourself.'

Bob laughed as he left the room to get the coffees. 'Take a pew,' he called back from the kitchen, 'I'll not be a minute.'

When Bob returned with the tray he went straight into his first line of enquiry. 'Did you bring the doughnuts?'

'Actually, I forgot.'

'Call yourself a partner, luckily Beccy dropped off some cheese scones earlier.'

'Did she know I was coming?'

'I told her I was going to invite you. That's why the place looks so clean. For a classy lady she's a dab hand at the housework. Talking about ladies, how are you getting on with Valerie, or should I not ask?'

'Okay.'

Bob knew from his friend's non-committal answer it was the end of that conversation so changed the subject. 'How do you think we're doing Tod?

'You and me?'

'The business, if we can call it that.'

'I don't know what you mean, "if we can call it that".

If my memory serves me well we were responsible for the arrest and incarceration of a few well-known gentleman, if not so well-known paedophile, were we not? And what about the Fort case, that certainly put the wind up the authorities and others, am I right?'

'Yes, and all pro bono, while we were funded by Rebecca. We've not made one penny from our work.'

'Is she complaining?'

'As a matter of fact, she is. Not because of the funding so much as the fact that we have not focussed on finding Sophie, which is a bit ironic don't you think, considering how much money Rebecca has put into the business.'

'But she's got the money. She's got more money and property than you and I have ever seen and more than we could ever imagine.'

'That's not the point Tod. The most important thing to her is not her wealth, it's her daughter and it's time we tried to find her!'

'You and Sophie got quite close during the investigation into her father's death. What actually went on there Bob? Are you privy to something that we know nothing about? She was treating you like a father figure, wasn't she? What did she tell you?'

Bob opened the conservatory door and walked

onto the patio. There was no sign of the snowdrops he'd planted to remind him of that moment in the Botanic Gardens when Sophie had told him about the abuse by her father. Those fragile flowers had long disappeared too.

Tod walked up behind him. 'Was it bad?'

'Aye, it was, and she was just a wee girl too.'

'I'm sorry Bob, I didn't know.' Tod walked over to the water-feature and turned to face his friend. 'We'll find her once we've put this stupid conspiracy theory to bed.'

'I don't think putting it to bed is going to be easy. Police Scotland has drafted in officers from across the country, but still Edinburgh's streets are overflowing with smack. I'm not involved of course as my role was with the Cauld Case Squad and that's been put on hold.'

'Well there's no conflict of interest now then is there? Get yourself back into the office and concentrate on JP Associates; I'm sure Tracey will enjoy you being there. In the meantime, you can tell Rebecca that we are going to find Sophie when this job is completed. Tell her if we don't finish this job a great many young lives will be ruined.'

'I suppose that will do to be getting on with,' said Bob. 'I'll phone Callum and get him to arrange for Sandy Grassick to take us over to Methil in his boat. That way we can get up close alongside the HMV Telemachus, if it is there. Sandy will be able to tell us whether he believes it looks seaworthy enough to be involved in drug importing. I've got to say though that I do doubt that very much. It is far too coincidental that the same ship used by Stewart is being used again.'

Tod hadn't seen the big man as focussed for some time and liked what he saw. 'I'll give Tracey and Harry the good news about our decision to find Sophie. You want to speak to Beccy. In the meantime, didn't you say we were going for a drink?'

CHAPTER TWENTY-THREE

Thursday 11th December

The Firth of Forth had looked as calm as Bob, Tod, Callum and Harry could remember when they were climbing aboard Sandy's lobster boat. Harry seemed the most nervous, but Tod had put that down to this being the first time he'd been out the house since being assaulted. Bob didn't look comfortable either, but then he was never much of a seafarer.

'You're looking a wee bit peaky Bob,' said Callum, 'a rough night last night?'

'No. The last time I was on a boat was on St. Mary's Loch when I was a boy and I was sea-sick then and that was only a rowing boat.'

'A'm not that keen either,' added Harry. 'What dae ye need me for anyway?'

'One never knows Harry,' said Tod, just glad that he'd been able to talk Harry into leaving the house.

As he said this he noticed Bob was looking back across the harbour to the main road. 'Just a minute,' he said. 'I think that's Rebecca's Range Rover.' It was, and Rebecca and her Uncle Peter were climbing out of it.

'You didn't tell us Rebecca was coming Bob,' said Tod, uneasily. It wasn't really Rebecca he minded though: it was Uncle Peter. Tod had only met him once

229

and that was in the office. He'd taken an instant dislike to the man then and that feeling returned when he saw him by the harbour.

'I didn't know. I told her we were going but didn't expect her to turn up.'

Peter handed down a large picnic basket to Bob. 'My niece insisted,' he said.

Sandy was smiling broadly as he guided the boat through the narrow entrance between the lighthouse and the breakwater. 'Glad to have you all aboard,' he said. 'I think we're in for a calm crossing, so no need to worry in that regard.' As he said this a small wave hit the bow and the boat rose slightly.

Both Bob and Harry grabbed hold of the rail. 'Could you not calm the waters for them Callum?' suggested Tod.

'Where did you get your sea legs Tod?' Callum replied.

'It's a long story but my ex-wife's parents owned a large yacht on the Solent.'

'Richard and I used to charter a yacht and sail around the isla...' Before she'd finished her sentence, Rebecca remembered what the others knew of her deceased husband. She sat down on the bench at the stern and became silent.

Bob struggled over to her holding the rail as he did so. 'Is that a picnic you have in there?' he asked, pointing to the basket.

She didn't answer.

'We're a wee bit full to overflowing ladies and gents,' said Sandy, 'so if you'd kindly spread your weight evenly we should have a smooth enough trip.' He removed a bottle of pills from his jacket pocket. 'Harry, take one of these, it should do the trick.'

Harry swallowed the pill but kept one hand firmly on the guardrail.

The boat made good speed across the Forth, only changing direction once to avoid the course of an ocean-going oil tanker on its way to Grangemouth. When they arrived at Methil harbour Sandy took the craft between the long breakwater and the wooden pier. Everyone on board was looking out for sight of the Telemachus when Callum spotted a deep-sea supply ship docked up near the town head.

He instructed Sandy to pull alongside the tall rusting ship. Sandy complied, the old car tyres tied around Sandy's boat taking the strain of the collision. Nearly everyone on board staggered slightly on impact, all except Harry who had miraculously found his sea legs during the crossing.

'What do you think,' Callum asked, 'Is that ship seaworthy Sandy?'

'Not a chance. Take a look at that anchor, it has seen better days. It wouldn't hold a rubber duck in a bath. You wouldn't get me going to sea in it, that's for sure. I think you'll find she's not sailed for wee while. Why don't you ask that auld fellow over there; from the looks of him he'll ken whether it has left harbour recently.'

The elderly man was fishing the harbour just off to the side of Telemachus. Rebecca offered to get the information they needed, and Sandy took his boat to the harbour side and moored against an ancient wooden ladder. After a few minutes Rebecca returned with the news that the Telemachus had not left harbour since its arrival in Methil years earlier and that its next destination was Inverkeithing breaker's yard. A silence fell over the boat's company. It was only broken when Peter suggested eating the picnic. He opened the basket to reveal a plethora of alcoholic beverages.

'A'll have the champagne,' said Harry cheerily.

'Where's the food?' asked Tod, 'I'm starvacious.'

'I thought I'd treat us all to fish and chips in Anstruther,' said Rebecca, 'that's if you don't mind adding another nautical mile or two onto our journey Sandy?'

'I was going to suggest the same myself,' he replied. 'I'll just get turned around and we'll be there in no time. Is that alright with you Harry?'

Harry had found the paper cups and had already popped a cork. 'Aye, nae bother Skipper.'

It was mid-afternoon before the lobster boat arrived back in Newhaven. Tod was hoping to get to the office to see Tracey to give her the run down on their journey while Harry was hoping to avoid her as he was full of the drink. He made his way to the Harbour Inn. Bob, Peter and Rebecca decided to go elsewhere.

If Tod had known Valerie was in the office with Tracey, he might have got a spurt on but he didn't, so saw no harm in accompanying Harry for one for the road.

Callum stayed behind with Sandy, the two old servicemen sitting at the stern of the boat finishing off the beer that Rebecca had kindly included in her basket.

Valerie had arrived at the office around lunchtime, looking for Tod to treat him to lunch. With no sign of him she treated Tracey to a carry-out. The two women got on very well and discussed their pasts and possible futures. When the conversation turned to art, Tracey asked about the painting which hung on their office wall.

'I've got a room with a view,' Valerie answered. 'When we were decanted from the Fort I was given a flat on the Waterfront. The panorama is to die for, so I spend a lot of time painting the changing scene in all its seasons.'

'Tod says your work is quite political. He says it's referring to a dying past and a desolate future for Scotland,' said Tracey.

'Oh, is that what Dougal says?'

'Dougal?'

'Dougal Douglas, from Muriel Spark's Ballad of Peckham Rye.'

'Don't know it,' said Tracey.

'You'll see what I mean if you read it.'

They moved closer to the painting and Tracey began pointing out familiar sights. 'A think that's the fishing boat they're away on today.'

'It probably is. It's seen better days, but the old skipper seems to know his stuff.'

'What's in the baskets?' asked Tracey.

'They're not baskets, they're lobster creels; it will be

lobsters or crabs. He does well. They're only on the quay a few minutes before a van arrives to take them to market.'

'Have you met him?'

'No.'

'You'll need to watch out then; if you were a photographer you could get done for taking an image without permission.' Tracey was getting her own back for being corrected about the creels.

'How do you know about that?' asked Valerie.

'Ma man Harry kens aw about that stuff. He teaches law at the community centre around the corner.'

The subject of art ended, and Tracey was about to get her coat when the door opened and Tod appeared.

'What, leaving early Moneypenny?'

'You've been drinking boss,' she replied. 'But that's not a bad impersonation of Bob James.'

'You don't grudge a man a wee drink now, do you?'

'No, but Valerie might have something to say about it Dougal; she's in the loo.'

CHAPTER TWENTY-FOUR

Friday 12th December

Having recovered slightly from his embarrassment at being found with a drink in him by Valerie, Tod finished off the day by treating her to an alcohol-free dinner at a local Indian restaurant. The evening went well though he was exhausted by nine o'clock and had to give his apologies.

He was still feeling slightly guilty the next morning as he stepped off the number 11 bus on Princes Street and headed for Waverley Station. Daniel was in his usual spot and seemed to be enjoying the company of passing commuters as they stopped to give him their philosophical thoughts on homelessness and other sundries. This suited Daniel in more ways than one and his old bush hat was already half-full of notes.

'Have you seen the gent who accosted you recently?' asked Tod, sitting down. 'You know, the one who no longer has his top of the range smart-phone?'

'I believe he is taking the train at Haymarket Station now,' answered Daniel.

Tod handed him the phone. 'I was going to nip into the gardens and give it to Janet myself but thought better of it.'

'Just as well, you wouldn't have found her there.'

'Has something happened to her?' Tod asked with genuine concern.

'It sure has. Her parents turned up and asked her to come home with them. She accepted.'

'How did they know where to find her? Oh, don't bother to answer that, I think I may know.'

'How did you get on speaking with Toby?'

'I haven't tried yet.'

'If I were you Tod, I'd probably give it a miss. He'll grow out of it, we all do, eventually.'

'Yes, maybe. Listen I need to speak to you about our recent case.'

'What, about Peter? I thought you were going to approach him yourself?'

'I'm still not convinced he's on our side. This Shifty Stewart business is really bothering me too.'

'Have you spoken with the famed Jimmy McGuire?'

'Bob has. I believe you had brief run-ins with Jimmy in the past.'

'You could say that. He was one evil bastard, and his off-spring were no better. Anyway, he knew Stewart in prison. They were bosom buddies I believe.'

'For someone who had only heard about Stewart at team meetings Daniel, you are fairly up to the mark with the goings on between him and McGuire.'

'I made it my business to know once you'd informed me that JP Associates was investigating a case that may or may not involve him. If you are involved in that case, then by proxy so is Valerie. Once I knew that, I made it my business to know all about McGuire and Stewart and about you and your associates. What I discovered is that there are as many skeletons in JP's closet as there are associates.'

Tod stood up and looked down at the homeless man for a few moments. 'I can't believe I'm standing here speaking with a tramp who sounds more like he's on active duty with MI5. Where do you get your information and what have you found out Daniel?'

'That's top secret I'm afraid. Let's just say I have a full dossier on each of you and on McGuire and Stewart.'

Tod walked away from Daniel then turned back. 'You may or may not know what I am capable of but there is one thing I can assure you. I will not be threatened by you, or any of your like.'

'Whatever you are thinking Tod, I can tell you it's not worth the worry. I stayed around here for Valerie's benefit and it's paid off for me too. Your being here is of benefit to me, I can assure you, no matter what you think.'

'And what benefit has being here brought you Daniel? You tried to intervene in politics that don't belong to you: you murdered your friend and colleague and now spend your days sponging off the Scottish public. And you have the audacity to think that Valerie cannot manage without you. What good does that do anyone?'

'You do have a such temper, for an ex-community worker Tod. Here's some good I can do you: I can tell you that McGuire is not involved in your case. Yes, he did ask for the port office workers to be made aware that if Harry was harmed they'd pay for it. He was a friend of Stewart but that was the past; he really has found God and is a changed man. Tracey is right about him. Peter Blue is here because he has retired. He may be of some use to you though and you can trust him. His ex-military colleague Callum, he's another story completely. I would be very careful how you handle him.'

'Is this to do with the fact he likes Valerie?'

'No, it's to do with what he is capable of. Anyway, enough of that, it will out. As far as the port authority is concerned, they have nothing whatsoever to do with illegal imports. There's no need to be, they make enough legitimately. I can tell you one thing about them though: there was a rumour that the office manager had a penchant for young men, not that that had anything to do with his murder, as far as I know.'

Tod turned his attention from Daniel and watched a train pull into the station. 'What is the answer Daniel? The streets of Edinburgh are awash with drugs and maybe, just maybe, they are coming in through Leith, and we are no further forward.'

'I'm sorry, I can't help you. How was your trip to Methil yesterday? Did that produce anything?'

'Yes, a severe headache for me, but apart from that, absolutely zilch.'

'Maybe you'd be better concentrating on finding Sophie?'

'Daniel, I don't believe this! How are you getting all this information?'

'Oh, come on Tod, why do you think they call us spooks?'

CHAPTER TWENTY-FIVE

Wednesday 17th December

Tod called a crisis meeting of the associates for twelve-thirty. Everyone was invited, and all said they could make it. Bob and Rebecca were last in, much to the pleasure of Tracey who quickly let them know all about punctuality and dedication. That was until she saw the bag of food in Rebecca's hand. Rebecca caught her surprise. 'I wanted to go more up-market, but Bob said it was time I got to know the earthier tastes. That was after he checked my attire to make sure I didn't offend anyone in Leith.' She put the bag on the coffee table.

Tracey spotted another opportunity. 'So, you've decided to grace us with your presence Mister James.'

'I was reminded by my partner Mr Peterson only the other day, that this is where my priorities lie.'

'In that case I'd better put the kettle on,' said Tracey. 'Mark, do you want to give me a hand.'

'What's all this about?' asked Jake. 'I havenae heard from ye for ages and now A'm called tae another board meeting.'

'We'll wait till everyone is seated before I begin,' said Tod.

'Callum, dae you want tea or coffee?' came a cry from the kitchen.

241

The call woke Callum from his reverie. He'd been staring at Valerie's painting. 'That will do nicely!' he shouted.

'Which?'

'Oh sorry, coffee!'

Once Tracey and Mark had returned with the drinks, Jake took the paper bags from the carrier-bag and tore each one open. 'Did ye have tae pay five pence for that carrier hen?' he asked Rebecca.

'Yes.'

'You'll never get rich that way. Ye should always carry a wee bag in that designer handbag. It could save ye a fortune.'

'I should do that really,' answered Rebecca, smiling.

'When you have finished giving Rebecca a lesson on how to get rich quick, Jake, maybe we could get down to the business in hand,' said Bob.

'That's what we've been waiting for!' answered Tracey, on Jake's behalf.

'Aye get on with it Tod, we've people to meet and places to go,' added Jake.

'Right. After some serious thinking and much research, it is with some regret we have decided to abandon the investigation into Bayani's revelation.'

'Would that be the grand, hooded phantom oft spoken of we are giving up and would that be the "royal we?"' asked Jake. 'Fae what A can remember, A've not been consulted.'

'Bob and I have decided that from now we are going to concentrate all our efforts on finding Sophie.'

'That's a new one on me,' said Bob. 'I was of the understanding that we were going to tackle the drugs job before looking for Sophie?'

'And A was of the impression that it wisnae just you and Bob that would be looking for Sophie,' said Tracey. 'Harry and I are involved tae, isn't that right Rebecca.'

'Aye, that's right,' added Harry.

'Yes, that is correct,' answered Rebecca.

'Do you have any thoughts on the matter Mark?' asked Tod, 'everyone else seems to.'

'As a matter of fact, I do. Although we haven't struck lucky as far as the drug imports are concerned, we do seem to be getting nearer to finding out what, if anything, is coming into Leith illegally. The trip which Callum and I made to the docks certainly showed that it is possible.' Mark looked at Callum, who was continuing to stare at Valerie's painting.

Bob joined in. 'I see where Tod is coming from with this. Police Scotland has put a great many of its limited resources at solving the drug problem and with Sandra Laing in charge it is only a matter of time until that happens. The national drug enforcement agencies are also involved along with police forces from across the UK. Perhaps it is time for JP Associates to concentrate its limited resources elsewhere, and finding Sophie is a priority.' Bob leaned back against his chair.

'Hey big man,' said Jake, 'A thought you were the original dog wie a bone. You'd have never given up on an enquiry before. It was because of that we solved the Fort case.'

'Might I remind you Jake that we didn't actually solve the Fort case and as far as the Bayani case is concerned, there isn't one. We are still working on mere conspiracy.'

'Are ye sure you're not just trying tae please somebody not too far fae here?'

Bob stood and walked around the group till he was directly behind Jake. 'Say anything like that again Jake and you might find yourself in bother,' he whispered into Jake's ear.

'Right everyone, I called this meeting to let you know of our decision,' intervened Tod before Jake could react. 'It's not up for discussion but I took it upon myself to let you know. As from tomorrow, we'll be turning all our energies towards finding Sophie.' Tod didn't add, if she is still alive.

It seemed to everyone that for the moment there was nothing more to be said and everyone except Tracey, Tod and Callum left the office.

'That was a bit harsh Tod. They mean well and have put a lot of their time into helping you. You might have heard them out some more before dismissing them out of hand.'

'Didn't you see what was happening Callum? If you'd spent less time admiring Valerie's work and more time focussing on the meeting you would have. Given another minute, Bob might have set about Jake, or vice-versa. No Callum, Bayani's conspiracy is going nowhere and I'm beginning to regret ever having gone to that ship. The only way to get that through to them was to be upfront and that goes for you too. Now if you don't mind, I've some real work to be getting on with.'

CHAPTER TWENTY-SIX

Thursday 18th December

Callum Mackie didn't sleep much that night and was up very early next morning. He'd spent the whole time trying to come to terms with what he had discovered. Skipping breakfast, he got dressed in gardening gear, but instead of going to the conservatory, his usual morning haunt, he headed out of the front door and down the steep hill to the sea wall. Everything was eerily quiet when he got there, and the sea was like a mirror.

In the past he'd found himself in a great many situations that most would rather run from, but he'd thought those days were behind him. Joining the ministry had helped in the process. During that time, he'd learned that benevolent approaches to conflict were more beneficial, but now he had the awful feeling that what he was about to confront could not have that effect. He turned towards Newhaven Harbour.

Sandy Grassick was busy filling his fuel tank when he saw Callum walking down the pontoon.

'My goodness Minister, you're up bright and early this morning.'

'What is it they say Sandy, it's the early bird that catches the worm, or in your case the lobster.'

'Aye, and if I don't get those pots in before the weather turns, the most I'll be catching is a cold. Have you seen the forecast?'

'Aye, I believe it's to get rough out there later.'

Sandy emptied the last of the diesel into the tank and laid the container on the pontoon. 'I'll pick that up on the way in. Anyway, what can I do for you?'

'I really enjoyed that wee trip out on the Forth last week. It fair took me back.'

'Where, to the Falklands?'

'Aye, indeed. Tell me Sandy, do you ever think about our time there and what we did?'

'Aye that I do, but there's nothing to question about it, is there? We freed the islands and gave the islanders back their land. You may, but I don't have any regrets, other than for the poor men who got caught up on the Sir Galahad. That should never have happened, and I've always felt in part responsible. I couldn't get the officers to agree to get those men off the ship.'

'I remember. You were really torn up about that.' Callum stepped aboard. 'We'd better get going if we've to beat the storm. You wouldn't mind if I took a trip out with you this morning?'

'It would be a pleasure Callum, normally, but I have a busy schedule and no time for a blether this morning.

I've a large order to meet.'

'Actually, it's about our investigation. I was wondering which course, if any, a ship might take if it were to be bringing in elicit cargo. I thought a view from just off Leith might help.

Sandy was about to object then thought better of it, undid the mooring ropes, and guided the small fishing boat between the lighthouse and the west pier. They were only a few hundred metres out when they reached the first of the buoys anchoring Sandy's creels.

Callum was looking back towards the docks. 'Are you still making a good living Sandy?'

'Aye, it's even better since they cleaned up the Water of Leith and the Edinburgh Sewage. The Forth is as clean as I've seen it.'

'Does your catch go straight to market from the harbour?'

'There will be a pick-up waiting for me when we get back in. Within twenty-four hours my catch will be being enjoyed by the citizens of London and Paris and further afield.'

'Do you not get the local chefs coming to the harbour? I saw a programme on the TV where the skipper phones the restaurants and lets them know what he has, even before he's landed, and they're waiting for him.'

'I could do that, but I don't. My wholesaler takes care of the produce. I can't be doing with modern technology. By the way, you'd better put that on.' Sandy leaned into the cabin and pulled out a lifejacket.

'I see you don't wear one Sandy, but I see you've some high-viz vests hanging there.'

Sandy ignored Callum's reference to the vests. 'And here's me can't swim either. Did you know that most fishermen can't swim?'

'Aye, you told me that when we were in the Falklands. So why not a lifejacket?

'Have you ever seen a fisherman in a lifejacket?'

'Come to think of it, no I haven't. Anyway, you've no time for a blether. Are you not going to pull up that pot? I can't wait to see your first catch of the day.'

'I thought you were focused on the dock entrance?' Sandy pulled on the rope then let it go. 'Nothing there; I did wonder about that when I saw the bright moon last night. Did you know that the lobsters in the Forth prefer it when the evening is pitch black? That is when they come scurrying out from their rocks.'

'I didn't know that, but I do know it's not all that comes scurrying out in the dark. Can you tell just from pulling at the rope whether you've anything in the pot?'

'I've been doing this job man and boy and can tell exactly what I have in my pots without a look.'

Callum took hold of the rope and began pulling.

'What are you doing?' Sandy took a hold of his arm.

His friend ignored the question and continued to pull upward until the creel landed on the deck. Both men looked down at the tightly wrapped, white plastic bags in the pot. 'Must have been wet down there last night Sandy, your lobsters having started wearing sou'westers.'

Sandy was about to answer when Callum held up his hand. 'Don't say a word; I think I know the story. Let's see if I've got it right. When your wife died you blamed the authorities. You'd worked hard all your life, been a regular at the kirk, fought for your country and all in vain. All you'd asked in return was that you and Maggie could live out your life in peace and quiet, but that was taken away from you when she died so you blamed anyone and everyone you could, including the NHS, God, and me. Am I right?'

Sandy sat down. 'How did you know?'

'We can get to that. When did you decide to start paying everybody back for your grief Sandy?'

'I was so angry Callum; I would have done anything to have Maggie back. I gave up on you and the kirk and it was all I could do not to murder the doctor who'd missed a proper diagnosis. That would be about the same time after Shifty Stewart went to jail and Jimmy McGuire found his God in the same place. Their incarceration left a void in the market that was very quickly filled, and I was approached by the new business owners and asked if I'd like a share, if I helped bring the stuff in.'

Callum interrupted. 'And you agreed, not for the money but for mere revenge! Do you realise how much damage your cargo has done? There are young people all over this city living on the streets and worse because of what you bring in here.'

'Don't give me any more of your sermons Callum. My wife died because the system didn't take the time to investigate her illness properly. She was given a ten-minute appointment and painkillers. A month later she was dead. That same system that you so cherish, destroys lives every day and it destroyed Maggie's!'

'I was as sorry as the next man Sandy, but you know everyone makes mistakes and you can't take life into your own hands because of it.'

'Before you continue with any more of your sanctimonious lecture tell me, how did you find out?'

'The HMV Telemachus over in Methil. Your old comrade posing as an angler, I recognised from the Falklands and he said the ship had not left harbour for

251

years, yet the mooring ropes were clean, no mussels or seaweed on them. If the ship was there permanently those ropes would have been covered in sea life, but they weren't, they had recently been in use.'

'I should have guessed you'd notice.'

'Then there was Valerie's painting. You have an admirer living in the apartment block by Asda and she has been working from her window, painting you at work. It was from one of her paintings that I saw the lobster pots she'd painted; they should have been filled with blue lobsters but in the picture, they had something white inside. Also, the Telemachus was in the distance, moving away from the harbour. And the black pick-up truck was parked ashore, just by your boat. She's a very accurate artist, our Valerie.'

'I had no idea. Anyway, the truck doesn't belong to me, it belongs to our wee cartel and it's one of my mates who does the driving.'

'Tell me Sandy, it was those mates who beat up Harry Cowan, am I right? He was frightened to tell me he'd been beaten up by old men. And was it you and your cronies who killed the port office manager, a man with the wife and family? Why did your vengeance have to stretch that far?

'I needed to try to throw your associates off the scent and that man with the wife and family you talk about has been molesting my great-nephew.'

'What do you mean?'

'My great-nephew Steven works in his office. The boss-man was more interested in young boys than he ever was in his family. He tried it on once too often with the boy and he told me.'

'I noticed you'd visited the office when I saw your name in the office diary.' Callum shook his head and was silent for a few moments before continuing. 'So, you decided to gut him from end to end. You have become judge and jury Sandy; you and only you decide who is guilty and who should be punished.'

'If that is how you want to see it then that is exactly what I have become Callum. We'd be as well hauling in the rest of those pots; the market is waiting.'

'What about Bayani?'

'The Filipino from the coal ship? My nephew and I met him in Brewers having what he called his last supper. He knew my nephew from the docks. He said he was leaving that evening to return to his homeland. He'd had enough of life in the north.'

'Is that the truth?'

'I wouldn't lie to you Callum, not now. The coal trade is drying up and he didn't have much choice. We did get to discuss his conspiracy theory and your case before he left. Little did he know he was sitting with his grand-

hooded phantom that night. Anyway, I gave him some money for his trip home.'

'I'm struggling to get my head around this Sandy. You were an elder in my kirk and one of the most upstanding men I'd ever met if you must know and quite a role model for me personally. It was meeting you in the Falklands that eventually led me to give up the military and becoming a minister. What really happened to you? This is more than about Margaret?'

'It really was about Margaret; that is until I began looking around at the society we'd fought for; the one where achievements were measured out in progress for communities. Look at it now, everyone and everything is geared towards individual greed and desire. The physical world we come from is long gone and what we are left with is greedy, self-obsessed folk who can't even pass the time of day with you for staring at their I-pads. So yes, I decided that maybe filling them with drugs wasn't such a bad idea. At least it would give them something else to think about while satisfying their cravings.'

'There are no business owners, are there Sandy. It's you who's running the whole show with your old cronies from the navy. That pick-up is yours, isn't it? It's the one parked where Harry Cowan was beaten up by the men in those high-viz vests. Was that merely to throw us off the scent too? No, don't even bother answering that. Sandy, have you ever thought what

Maggie would have said about your venture had she been alive?'

'If Maggie had been alive there'd have been no venture.'

'How did you manage to talk your old friends into this?'

'That was easy enough. Like me they've worked hard all their lives and fought for their country, but when the chips came down and age hit them, they realised that no-one and I mean no-one, gave a toss whether they live or die. The ones who weren't yet incarcerated in a nursing home were more than happy to oblige. The angler on the pier at Methil is the skipper of the Telemachus. He takes her out once a week and moors just off Inchkeith Island where a larger, deep-sea vessel delivers our cargo. From there the boys moor off Leith and take the inflatable to fill my pots during the night.

'You've got it all worked out my old friend, with never a moment's remorse. We might as well bring in the rest of your catch.'

'Are you taking me in?'

'Something like that.'

Sandy put his hand forward to shake Callum's. That's when Callum noticed the tarantula tattoo on the back of his hand.

'A fitting tattoo Sandy, I must say.'

Ten minutes from the end of her shift Tracey was getting ready to go and was about to switch off the radio when an announcement caught her attention.

'Did you hear that boss?'

'What?' asked Tod.

'A Newhaven fisherman has been washed ashore on Portobello Beach. His lobster boat was found drifting earlier in the day by a port authority tug in the Forth. The sea was really rough they said, and they think he was washed overboard. He wisnae wearing a life jacket.'

Tod immediately phoned Callum but there was no answer.

On the way home that night, Tod stopped off at his corner shop for a newspaper, expecting to see the drowning as the main headline, but it had been relegated to the second page by a front-page exposé.

LARGE DRUG HAUL FOUND AFTER ANONYMOUS TIP-OFF. DRUGS, THOUGHT TO BE WORTH MILLIONS, WERE FOUND IN A BLACK PICK-UP TRUCK PARKED BY NEWHAVEN HARBOUR.

Detective Inspector Sandra Laing of Police Scotland's Project Aunt Nora, believes the haul may be part of a much bigger operation, centred around the Lothians and Fife.

The End

Glossary

Scots – English Translation

A	-	I
awfie	-	very
aye	-	yes
bam	-	stupid person
beat it	-	go away
blether	-	converse
cannae	-	can not
cauld	-	cold
clamjamfry	-	a mob, crowd or rabble
clarty	-	dirty
couldnae	-	could not
crabbit	-	bad tempered
daen	-	doing
daft	-	stupid person
dinnae	-	do not
eejit	-	stupid person

hadnae	-	had not
hame	-	home
havnae	-	have not
hen	-	term used in greeting a woman
heid	-	head
feart	-	frightened
gaun	-	go or going
gie	-	give
glaikit	-	stupid
gonnae	-	going to
guid	-	good
intae	-	into
jammy	-	lucky
lintie	-	linnet
ma	-	my
mair	-	more
maist	-	most
manky	-	dirty

masel	-	myself
na	-	no
nyaff	-	insignificant person, stupid, irritating
thegither	-	together
whae	-	who
widnae	-	would not
yin	-	one